Christmas Love Letters for Evie

Diane Burke

CHRISTMAS LOVE LETTERS FOR EVIE
Copyright © 2020 by Diane Burke

All rights reserved.

This book is a work of fiction. The characters, events, and places portrayed are products of the author's imagination and are either fictitious or used fictitiously. Any similarity to real persons, either living or dead, is purely coincidental and not intended by the author.

ISBN Paperback: 978-1-7330529-3-1
ISBN eBook: 978-1-7330529-4-8

Acknowledgments

Cover provided by Claudia Valcich Photography.

Heartfelt thanks to Claudia Valcich, Brenda Smith, and Monnie Brewster. I couldn't do it without you in my corner helping, advising and encouraging me every step of the way.

Also a big thank you to Sue Grimshaw, developmental editor, Claudia Valcich Photography for cover design, and Amy Atwell for formatting.

One

"No, Pug! No!" Eve Carlson chased the little thief as the dog slid under the dining room table, scrambling like he's on ice across the hardwood floor and making a mad dash toward the new living room carpet.

"No! Please, Pug. You'll get pizza sauce on the rug!" Eve pushed her legs into overdrive. She lost her balance and slid across the foyer, managing to catch the hind legs of the runaway pilferer seconds before he reached the end of the tile. She scooped up the squirming animal and held him tightly in her arms, the stolen piece of pizza squashed between the dog's belly and her chest. But she should have known that wouldn't stop *this* dog. He continued to squirm and chew and lick whatever he could pull into his mouth.

"What am I going to do with you?" She blew out a frustrated breath from her seated position on the floor. He was trying to adjust to their new normal as much as she was and she hated herself when she got mad at him, but it was like he was constantly testing her. Eve lowered him from her lap and held what was left of the slice in the air, up and out of his reach. "Bad dog, Pug. You know you're not supposed to steal food." She admonished him but her heart wasn't in it, he was hurting as much as she was.

As he sat down next to her, his intense stare warned her he was waiting for a second opportunity to grab the pizza.

Not looking the slightest bit contrite, Pug climbed onto her thigh and started licking the excess cheese from her shirt.

"Ohhhhhhh!" She gently nudged the dog away, stood up and stared down at the culprit. She studied the round black eyes and black short snout looking back at her. "Bryan should have named you Bandit. That name is much more appropriate than Pug, don't ya think?"

The dog made a rumbling sound in his throat letting her know he wasn't admitting defeat and still had pizza on the brain.

"Don't look at me like that. If you weren't so fat from all the food you steal, I wouldn't have been able to catch you. So it's your own fault."

Pug poked out his tongue and swiped it along his lips.

She pushed her bangs out of her eyes, shook her head, and headed back into the kitchen. The dog trotted behind, his nails clicking across the hardwood dining room floor.

Note to self. Dog needs nails trimmed.

She lifted the lid on the trash can only to have Pug make one last leap for the slice before she could get the lid back down.

"Stop that!"

Maybe I won't get your nails trimmed. That'll teach you. I'll let them grow so long it will be impossible for you to sneak up on anyone and steal food.

She walked over to the dog dishes and pointed her index finger toward the floor. "Look! You have plenty of food in this bowl. And what about this one? This bowl is filled with fresh spring water—not tap water, mind you—spring water. I'm treating you like a king. A little gratitude would go a long way, buddy."

Pug ignored her and circled the trash can.

Eve fisted her hands on her jean-clad hips. "Okay, maybe gratitude is too much to expect. I'll settle for a simple wag of your tail. Try it. You might actually like it."

The dog became selectively deaf and continued to ignore her as he sniffed at the base of the trash can.

Eve sighed. Almost a year had passed since she inherited this dog and he was no closer to liking her than he had ever been. She got so frustrated that sometimes she wished she could find him another owner. Sometimes. But she knew she never would. Bryan loved this dog. This inheritance wasn't being forfeited, ever.

She watched the dog circling the trash can and shook her head. Pug had always loved food, but this past year he was almost insatiable. She guessed everyone handles grief in their own way, even dogs she supposed.

"I know, boy. I miss him, too."

Eve glanced out the kitchen window at the wintry Pennsylvania landscape. Christmas was less than four weeks away. Bryan and she had always loved this time of year. They went crazy with holiday decorations, and music, and dressing in different Christmas outfits each week of December. Bryan had dressed Pug, too, in a variety of holiday sweaters. Once he'd even donned Pug in a tiny Santa hat and attached a wisp of a white beard to his chin.

But the funniest get-up of all was the time Bryan had found a plastic headband holding reindeer ears. Pug hated those ears. He grumbled and scowled and whined each time he had to wear them. But he wore them. Pug would do anything for Bryan. He loved and obeyed his royal lord and master without question.

Eve sighed. Fat chance the dog would let her anywhere near him with reindeer ears this year. She'd probably lose a finger or two if she tried. Boy, oh boy, that dog had loved Bryan.

But last year Bryan had done the unthinkable. He'd died the day after Christmas.

And the world had stopped.

For both of them.

Pug had always been Bryan's dog. Dog and man had forged a tight, special bond and the dog had never truly warmed up to her. He simply tolerated her. No matter what she did or how hard she tried. But she understood. She wasn't Bryan. And even now, almost a year after his death, Pug still slept every night at the base of the front door waiting for Bryan to come home.

Maybe that's why she hadn't given up on the dog. She understood. Sometimes on a particularly lonely, hard night she would sit in the dark on the top step, stare down at the front door and hope, just for one moment, Pug knew something she didn't and Bryan would come through that door.

But he didn't.

What did that make her? Crazy? Lonely? Heartbroken?

Yep. All of it and more.

No longer hungry, Eve wrapped her remaining piece of pizza on a plate and slid it into the refrigerator for another day. She cleaned the couple of dirty glasses gathering in the sink, swiped at the kitchen counters, then turned and frowned at Pug one more time.

"Okay, Pug. Lights off. Kitchen closed. I'll leave your food down. You'll eat when your dog food when you get hungry. I'm not going to worry about it."

Flipping the light switch, she moved from the darkened kitchen into the den. She plopped down on the leather sofa, tucked her legs up, and grabbed the book on the side table. No matter how hard she tried to concentrate or how many five-star ratings this book had earned, she just couldn't get into the story. After reading the same page twice, she placed a book mark in her spot and set it back on the table.

Her eyes moved to the dormant fireplace across the room. Tonight would be a perfect night for a fire. She could see a sprinkling of snowflakes hitting the window panes. It was a gas fireplace with fake but realistic logs so lighting a fire surely wouldn't be difficult. But, for some reason, she couldn't make herself cross the room to do it.

Bryan started the fire each evening. While she made them a snack tray of cheese, crackers, and wine. Tonight, she sat only with a solitary glass of wine.

Enough said.

Sighing deeply, she tried to distract herself with the age-old king of distractors, the TV remote control. She flipped the channels like a film reel out of control as talk shows, canned comedy sitcoms, infomercials, and news programs flashed across the screen. It said a lot about her crabby mood tonight when her thumb hit the off button and a wave of relief washed over her as she stared at the blank screen.

But that relief lasted only as long as it took for Eve to raise her eyes to the picture above the fireplace. Her eyes felt glued to the young, hopeful, trusting, smiling faces staring back at her. They were all dressed up in their wedding finery and believed the world was theirs for the taking and happily-ever-after's happened in real life, too, not just in fairy tales.

And they'd been happy…ecstatically, unbelievably happy.

Until they weren't.

Eve sipped her wine and did something she hadn't allowed herself to do for months. She allowed her mind and heart to travel back to better days.

She'd married Bryan in December surrounded by friends and family in a beautiful chapel decorated with Christmas poinsettias, pine greenery, white lights and candlelight. Eve had worn a white gown with white fur edging the beautiful satin hood, the scoop neckline and the end of both long sleeves. She carried a white fur muff instead of flowers. She felt like a maiden out of Camelot. She felt beautiful…special…and she knew she'd never feel as beautiful again.

Eve had walked alone up the aisle, her dad present in spirit only after a car accident had claimed his life years before, and she wed her life-long best friend, Bryan Thomas Carlton.

Her eyes moistened and tears threatened to overflow, again. She refused to break down. No matter what, she would never regret becoming Bryan's wife. Bryan's widow—that was an entirely different story.

A small, melancholy smile crossed her lips as the sound of his voice filled her memories.

"I don't know what I'd ever do without you, Evie. You're like the other half of me…the better half."

Evie.

He was the only person who had ever called her Evie. It was his special nickname for her, particularly at this time of year, when he'd call her his very special Christmas Evie for the first time.

She sighed heavily, her grief still fresh even a year later, still feeling like she wore a heavy weight that might never lift. Evie had died with Bryan that day and only a caricature of a person named Eve had been left behind. A caricature who couldn't seem to find her way, couldn't navigate this pain, couldn't figure out what was to become of her now since the other half of her was gone.

And Bryan had, indeed, been the other half of her. They began as childhood pals. Hung out as teenage friends. Became married lovers—for thirteen wonderful years—until cancer came calling and stole the love of her life away. And herself? She'd spent the past year of her life trying to figure out how one half of a person, burdened with a broken and shattered heart, gets through a day when their other half is gone?

So far she had more questions than answers. Taking care of Pug—the dog her husband had named after its breed, despite a million other suggestions, and loved almost as much as he'd loved her—got her through some of the tougher times.

Still.

She stared out the window a few minutes more hoping she'd feel anything, a spark of hope, the tiniest niggling of Christmas cheer, but she didn't. She felt empty. Numb. Lost.

Pug's whimpering brought her back to the present. "What?" She stared down at the dog hovering in the doorway. Pug would never cross over to her. He'd keep her in sight, lying at the edges of whatever room she was in, but he'd never come close enough to offer any affection. Punishment, doggie style, she supposed.

"Do you need to go out?" she asked. The dog simply looked at her and whined some more. She got up, grabbed the leash hanging by the back door and shook it. "Hey, Pug, do you want to go for a ride in the truck? Huh? Go to the park?"

Pug, probably still mad at her for stealing the pizza back, threw her a look that could only be interpreted as "Not if it means riding with you."

"Okay, Pug. Have it your way." Eve opened the back door, stepped outside and before she could close the door behind her, the dog darted through her legs, slid on a patch of ice on the sidewalk and came to a face-splat stop against a snowdrift.

Eve laughed, snapped the leash onto his collar, and then picked him up and carried him to the truck. The huge truck. The monster truck. The truck she could never understand why they bought. Bryan's truck.

She didn't drive it often. It was too big for her and that made her nervous. She liked her little Honda Fit just fine. But riding in the truck calmed Pug down. He loved the truck almost as much as Bryan had. So she opened the door and gently tossed him into the back seat.

The dog took his favorite spot, leaned his front paws on the window, and pressed his face against the glass. Pug loved hanging his head out the window. Letting the wind blow in his face was his number one favorite activity in life. Second, of course, only to stealing people food every chance he got. This conscious-less mutt literally stole food from a baby once. That was the one and only time Bryan had scolded the dog for his misbehavior and then he'd bought the baby and her entire family a second ice cream cone as an apology.

Who knew Pug couldn't resist ice cream?

But this wasn't summer. And it was too cold to roll the window down no matter how much whimpering Pug did. He'd have to be happy with the ride and looking out the glass. After how he'd behaved, he was lucky she was taking him for a ride at all. She headed to the park almost on auto pilot, her thoughts on the many times Bryan had taken them there.

They stayed in the park longer than she'd anticipated. Pug had managed to find an infinite amount of new smell spots to mark his territory despite the snow. And she'd gotten caught up watching the kids skating on the pond. Skating was something she'd never learned how to do but had always wanted to learn. Gliding across the ice. Arms wide. Spinning. Free. Flying.

Bryan had promised to teach her. It was the only promise he'd ever made to her that he hadn't kept.

That and the promise to never leave her.

"C'mon, Pug. Let's go home." She pushed the memories from her mind, tugged on the leash and headed back to the truck. The pink, purple and blue colors of the sunset over the pond were stunning and she paused for a few more minutes to enjoy them. She hoped the ride had lightened Pug's heart because it didn't seem anything, even something as beautiful as this sunset, could lighten either of their hearts this holiday season. Slowly, she backed out of the parking spot and started for home.

It didn't take long for Pug to start the whining and crying because the window wasn't down.

"Doggone it, Pug. You are the most spoiled animal that ever lived!" Eve threw the temperature control on the heater to high, pulled her winter coat tighter, and lowered the back passenger window. The dog's hind end quivered with excitement as he hung his head out the window. She shivered in the front seat with pending frost bite despite the heater on high. But she decided she shouldn't be complaining to Pug about how spoiled he was when she was the one doing the spoiling.

She glanced back at the dog who, at the moment, seemed to be in heaven on earth. She chuckled. Bryan would have loved seeing his dog this happy—and that thought lightened her heart, too.

Michael McGruder hunkered down against the back of the truck cab, pulling his coat collar up around his neck and wrapping his arms around his coat.

Damn, it's cold!

What did he think it was going to feel like riding in the opened bed of a truck with a haul of evergreens for the Christmas tree lot? Thirty-two degrees outside today not counting the feel of the wind when the truck was moving. Why hadn't he followed in his own car?

Stupid. Stupid. Stupid.

As they approached the main traffic light leading into the heart of town, Michael could feel the truck slow, then speed up, then slow again, and he chuckled. His dad was obviously trying to make a last minute decision whether to try to beat the light or wait. This particular light was the longest light in a hundred mile radius. Everyone in town knew it. He'd actually timed it once. You get stuck at this light and you'd better hope there was a good song on the radio because you had at least a three minute wait before you'd see the color green again. Cows could cross the street faster than the cars could make it through this intersection. The truck crept to a stop and Michael chuckled. He knew that decision was killing his dad. If his granddaughter, Katie, wasn't sitting beside him, Michael was sure his dad would have made a run through the yellow light.

What did it matter anyway? It would give Katie a chance to look out the windshield and see straight down Main Street. It was just a couple days after Thanksgiving and already the streets bustled with shoppers. The wire arbor Newton Hills hung over the street every year was already decorated with garland and lights. Holly would be excited at the sight of the holiday preparations. He wished he could be sitting in the cab with them so he could see her expression. But, no, he had to be the better guy, offering that extra spot to his brother and volunteering to ride the short trip in the truck bed.

Yep. Stupid me.

As they pulled to a stop, the truck beside him threw a shadow over him. He turned and looked. Man, oh man, that was a big truck. He'd hate to ever have to change one of those giant tires. Why on earth would anyone own one of those monster trucks? As far as he knew, the only thing they were good for was racing in mud.

Trying to distract himself from the bitter cold, he turned his attention to the sack at his side, opened it, and pulled out a ham and turkey sandwich. Might as well put the extra time to good use. He no sooner lifted the sandwich to his lips and took a bite then it happened.

He caught the movement out of his peripheral vision. The monster truck was throwing something at him! Before he could move a muscle, the object knocked the sandwich out of his mouth and landed hard in his lap. He didn't know what part of his body was more surprised, his eyes that stared in astonishment at the animal eating his sandwich or his throbbing groin from the sudden impact of this fat dog.

"Oh my God, I'm so sorry. He's never, ever done something like that before. I didn't even know he could do something like that. He's a small, fat dog. I can't believe he did that!"

A petite, auburn-haired young woman frantically raced in circles right beneath the edge of his truck. She flailed her arms in the air as she circled and the astonishment on her face probably mirrored the one he was sure he wore.

This was a joke? A prank, right? How in the world...?

"Are you all right?" she asked, as her fingers wrapped around the edge of the truck bed and she kept hopping up and down to try and see inside.

He chuckled and looked over the side of his truck right into her green eyes, gorgeous, glittering, beautiful green eyes.

Yeah, his brother set this up as a prank. Okay, he'd play along.

"Good thing it was me sitting back here and not my dad. Having a dog leaping through the air at you out of nowhere isn't good for the heart," Michael said.

"Ohhh, I know. I'm so sorry." Eve stood on tip-toe and tried to reach up over the edge of the truck bed to grab the dog but she was too short. The dog jumped off his lap with sandwich in tow and made himself at home on the branches of a downed tree.

"Pug, get over here right now," she demanded.

The man laughed, grabbed up the dog, and hopped over the side of the truck to stand in front of her. He didn't know what surprised him more, how even prettier she was up close or how her errant dog snuggled contentedly in his arms like he belonged there.

"The way this dog went after my sandwich I'd swear you didn't feed him." Michael said, and offered her his best, forgiving smile. "But from the heft of this little guy, I'd say you probably feed him too much."

Both doors on the pick-up truck opened and two more men and a small girl rushed out.

"Did I see what I thought I saw?" A gentlemen, probably in his late sixties, was the first to join them. "I looked in my side-view mirror and could hardly believe my eyes. Who knew small dogs could fly?" He chuckled and patted Pug's head. The resemblance to the man holding her dog left no question that he must be the father.

"I wouldn't say he flew, Dad," Michael said. He glanced at the monster truck. "I'd say gravity had a lot to do with helping him make the leap. I'm glad our truck bed was enough to cushion the poor pup's landing—that and my lap, of course. Only thing truly hurt in this fiasco was my sandwich."

Katie pulled on Michael's coat. "Let me see, Daddy. Let me see the doggie." He scooted down so the girl could pet the dog. He couldn't believe it but it looked like the dog almost smiled.

A second man rounded the truck. "Hi," the young man said, offering his hand. "I'm Danny McGruder. If they haven't introduced themselves yet, this is my brother, Michael, my father, Sean, and my niece, Katie."

She shook his hand. "Hi. I'm Eve Carlson."

"And this must be the flying dog." Danny said, planting his fists on his hips and laughing out loud.

"Don't know how you set this up but it was one crazy prank," Michael said. "Good for you no one got hurt."

"Me?" Danny pointed a finger at his own chest. "You thought I set this up?" He laughed louder. "Hey, bro, I love to pull pranks but this one was too good even for me." He turned his attention back to Eve and her dog. "Boy, do we have a story to tell Mom."

Although the entire fiasco felt like only seconds had passed, the traffic light changed and the cars in both lanes started beeping their horns demanding they move.

"Looks like we've got to get moving. Here's your dog." Michael smiled and handed her the little food thief.

His dad, brother, and daughter hurried back to their seats.

"Again, I'm so sorry," she said, holding Pug tightly in her arms.

"Don't worry about it. It's not every day I have a fun story to tell."

He gave a mock salute and climbed up into the truck. He watched as Eve hurried around the back of her truck and disappeared. He couldn't believe this adorable, petite woman was even able to climb up in a truck this size, let alone drive one. He shook his head as he tried to absorb all that had happened in just a few minutes.

His dad, probably flustered by the sound of horns beeping and the fear of the light changing red again, must have floored the gas because their small truck shot off. Michael glanced up as they moved past the monster truck. All he could see was the dog's face plastered against the pane of a closed window.

A smile pulled at his lips as he puzzled things out. *God has a sense of humor doesn't he?* If he'd been following the truck with his car, he would never have had fat pug fly through the air and land in his lap. He laughed out loud and his smile grew into a full-fledged grin. This was one of those stories his family would tell around the dinner table in the years ahead, whenever they wanted to embarrass him or have a laugh. The look of sheer joy on his daughter's face when she actually got to pet the flying pug was precious. Certainly enough to make him toughen up and endure the remainder of this frigid trip. He settled his head back and inhaled the heavy scent of pine. Christmas, his favorite time of year, and the busiest. Despite a to-do list as long as this truck bed, he decided he was going to relax, try to ignore freezing to death, and enjoy the flying dog scenario once again.

He had to admit the flying pug hadn't been his only surprise. He had expected a big, burly truck driver to jump out of the monster truck cab. Yeah, okay, he knew in today's world, he'd probably be considered a walking Neanderthal because he still enjoyed opening doors for women and treating them like ladies. He was well aware women today could be found in every setting, every occupation, and doing a damn good job of it. He knew that.

But a monster truck?

He laughed again.

She'd been such a cute, petite, adorable creature. He couldn't believe she could even see over the steering wheel of that monster truck, let alone have the skills to maneuver the thing.

Eve Carlson. I bet there's many things about you I would find surprising and interesting. Yeah, like a big, burly husband to go along with that monster truck.

He shook his head and brought things back down to reality. He had no business daydreaming about a stranger. He wasn't a foolish kid. Quite the contrary. He'd passed his forty-fourth birthday just a few months ago. He chuckled. Hell, he was still dealing with the fact that he'd found his first gray hair, two if he was being honest.

Nope. He certainly wasn't a young, foolish kid with a crush. Those days were long gone.

But something about her intrigued him…and that hadn't happened since Susan.

Damn. Now why had he let his mind go there?

Two

"Hi, Mom. Of course, I'm not mad at you for going to Florida without me." She bit her lower lip and tried not to grin. "Mom, why would I be mad? I'm the one who insisted you go, remember?" She stifled a groan and held the phone away from her ear for a few seconds as her mother gave her a laundry list of why she shouldn't have listened to her and should have stayed with her this Christmas. Eve put the phone back to her ear. "Mom, we've been over this a dozen times. You have nothing to feel guilty about. I could have gone to Florida with you, remember? Matter of fact, both you and Connie were pretty persistent about it. I chose not to go."

Her mother was spending the holidays with her sister's family in Florida this year and it was a blessing. Not that she didn't love her mom, or her sister—she adored them both—but this year, the first Christmas season without Bryan, the last thing she needed was a helicopter mom or hovering sister.

"I know you wanted to stay with me, and I love you for it. I do." Eve softened her voice. "But you can't grieve for me, Mom. It's better for everyone that I have this time alone. Please, don't be upset." She smiled as she listened to her mom reassure her.

"Mom, I've got to go. I've got a million things on my list to get done today. Give Connie my love. Yes, I'll call tomorrow. I love you, too. Bye."

Her family missed Bryan, too.

Who wouldn't miss Bryan—the life of every party, the energy in a room, the kind, sweet, smart boy who became one hell of a man?

Eve set her coffee cup on the table and gazed out the window. It seemed like that was the main thing she did lately. Look at life outside the window instead of finding a way of living life again. But this time her eyes didn't focus on the landscape or the weather. Her mind was too busy. Twenty-six more days. Christmas would be over and the first anniversary of Bryan's death would have passed. If she could make it through a measly twenty-six more days, maybe she would be able to move forward instead of being mired in a quicksand of memories and pain.

Now all she had to do was believe it.

She washed the few dishes in the sink and placed them in the rack to air-dry. She made sure Pug's dishes were fresh and full. Where was he, anyway? She glanced around the kitchen and saw the dog sound asleep in a shaft of light coming through the window. She guessed his escapade of flying through the air from one truck to another wore him out because he'd been a perfect angel ever since yesterday's incident.

A smile tugged at her lips. Once the shock wore off, she'd found the whole thing absurdly funny. Thank God if Pug was going to do something this stupid, he'd picked a lovely family to do it to. They'd been so understanding. The little girl was adorable, and she giggled when Pug licked her hand. And the child's father—she hoped some lucky lady knew what a good man she'd married—and a handsome one to boot.

She shook her head to rid the image of sapphire blue eyes framed by laugh lines out of her memory. It wasn't like this was the first good looking guy she'd seen since losing Bryan. There were plenty of nice looking guys out there. And, Lord knows, she certainly wasn't in the market for another relationship. Sometimes she believed she'd never be and that was fine with her.

She had a good job. Michael's life insurance money had paid off their mortgage and enabled her to also save for a rainy day so she didn't have any immediate financial problems. Her mom lived close by and they visited often. Her friends stopped by regularly and Pug made sure she got her daily exercise. She was content.

After all the pain, content felt good.

So what was it about Michael?

She'd only taken notice of him because she'd been taken off guard. She hadn't been expecting…well, she hadn't been expecting anything. She barely noticed the people around her, male or female, handsome or not, anymore. The last year of Bryan's life had been long days and nights in hospital rooms and eventually hospice.

And this year…this year she'd grieved so deeply, so painfully, she didn't even notice her own reflection when she looked in the mirror.

So that's all it was. A momentary surprise of coming face to face with a gorgeous guy. It jump started something inside, something reminding her that she was still a woman and alive, whether she wanted to be or not. Instantly, a wave of guilt swept over her and she did her best to brush it away. Bryan would never have wanted her to feel guilty or depressed about anything. She knew that. Still…

A mental image of Bryan's face—grinning at her, teasing her—filled her mind and she smiled. After his death, Eve hadn't thought she'd ever have any reason to smile again. Her grief had overwhelmed her and she'd almost drowned in it.

But she smiled yesterday. She actually laughed out loud at one of Pug's antics. And later that evening, she'd smiled when she'd spent some time looking at past Christmas photos. She found herself smiling again today, for simply no reason at all, and somehow she knew that would have made Bryan happy. He loved to make her laugh.

She knew what would have made him unhappy, too. Ignoring their holiday traditions this year by not decorating the house or even getting a tree.

She'd thought trying to ignore the holiday might help ease the pain of trying to get through this month without him. She certainly didn't feel in a festive mood this year. But knowing how much both of them had loved the holidays, she felt pressed to do *something*…in memory of him.

She glanced over at Pug, making sure he still slept and wasn't into any mischief, and then headed to the bedroom. She crossed to the hope chest at the foot of her bed and lifted the lid. Nestled on the bottom, wrapped in tissue paper, was the ivory-colored Christmas afghan her grandmother had crocheted and given to them as a wedding gift. She cherished this afghan, especially since her grandmother wasn't with them any longer. But, also, because she cherished the memories of cuddling under the afghan enclosed in Bryan's arms, watching the Hallmark holiday movies. He always complained when she coaxed him to watch "chick flicks" but he hadn't fooled her. He enjoyed them as much as she did. He proved it with his own romantic gestures when the movies ended.

She lifted the blanket from the hope chest and closed the lid. Sitting on the edge of the bed, she discarded the tissue paper and ran her hands over the soft wool, taking particular note of the red crocheted poinsettias her grandmother had attached to the diagonal corners. She carried it out to the living room and opened it up. When she did, something slipped out of the folds of the blanket and fell to the floor. She spread the afghan across the back of the sofa and then looked down to see what had slipped out. Her eyes fell on a white envelope with Evie sprawled across the front and she froze. She recognized the handwriting and the nickname. The letter was from Bryan.

Her fingers shook as she leaned over and picked up the envelope. Her breath caught in her throat and her eyes smarted with tears. Her legs trembled and she sat down before she fell down. Taking a deep breath…and then another…she slid her fingernail beneath the seal and opened the letter.

Dear Eve,

I know this letter will come as a shock. No, it isn't a prank or a cruel joke. It's really me. I know you only pull this afghan out during the holidays so if you found this letter, then it is the Christmas season again. And you know me, I can't be left out of anything.

This will be your first Christmas without me. I know it will be hard. But I don't want it to be too hard, Evie. I want it to be special and fun, not only this year but for all the years to come.

I can't imagine how I would be feeling right now if the situation had been reversed and I was facing life without you. I don't think I could do it. But you can. We both know women are stronger than men in so many ways. Remember the debates we had over cave men tactics versus being able to cry in public? Men can strengthen their biceps, protect their women, and provide for their families. But we stink at all the heart-felt things, don't we? Women beat us every time in those arenas. That's one of the many things I admire and love about you. You're independent, confident, and strong. So be strong now, honey. Please.

Forgive me for causing you pain. You know if I could have stayed, I would have.

But it is what it is.

I don't want you to go through your first holiday season alone. I know you're probably not really alone. I bet your mom and sister are probably smothering you with kindness. Try to remember they only want to help.

I want to be there with you, too. I want to help you through the loss of us. And the only way I can think to do that, under the circumstances, is to take this time to remind you of all the many reasons we were in love.

Our picnics in Sumter Park, riding bikes, pulling pranks (remember the time we strung toilet paper all over Principal Hinson's trees and shrubs at Halloween? It was embarrassing because we weren't kids anymore and we got caught but it was worth it just to see the expression on his face, wasn't it? What an mean old man!) Bowling on every third Saturday. The card games with our families. And, yeah, watching year after year of Survivor. Can you believe how hooked we were on that show?

There were plenty of other great times, too. Remember the time you dragged me to a cooking class with you and then got mad when I turned out to be a better cook. I'm still laughing at that one.

So many memories. Big things. Buying our first house. Taking great vacations.

Oh yeah, and don't forget the little things, the everyday things. Reading together in front of the fireplace on a cold winter's night. Working side-by-side in our garden. Sharing a bubble bath by candlelight in our garden tub and after... Yeah, I'm grinning over those memories, too.

I'm hoping you're smiling with me right now. That's what I want, Evie. I want you to be happy. I love you—with all my heart. I will love you forever, even death can't take that away.

Eve dropped the letter to her lap. "I love you, too, Bryan," she whispered into empty air. She covered her face with her hands and choked on a sob. Bryan knew her so well. Only Bryan would know what this letter would mean to her and, sick as he was, he still found the strength and time to write it…and then hide it. How the heck did he manage that? She smiled through her tears, then picked up the letter again.

Okay, Evie, take a breath. I know I needed to stop a couple of times while writing this. Who says men don't cry? LOL Seriously, though, are you okay? Good. Now dry those tears, sit back and listen. Close your eyes and listen hard, Evie.

Can you hear me laughing?

I am, you know.

I can picture the expression on your face as you try to figure out when I wrote this letter and how it got into your Grandmother's afghan.

I'm right. Right?

I'm laughing, Evie. I hope you are, too. That's one of the things we did so well together, laughed. We found joy and humor and blessings in each day and in each other. I pray you never lose the gift of laughter.

When I knew our time together was almost over, I wrote this letter and slipped it into your grandmother's afghan. You didn't make it easy, you know. I had to come up with one request after another to get you to leave my side long enough to get this darn thing written. But I managed. Then I snuck into our room and tucked it into the blanket after you'd fallen asleep. I knew you'd find it when you pulled the blanket out. What better place to start a conversation with you than wrapped up in the blanket we used to wrap up in together and watch those sappy romance movies?

Yeah, yeah. I hear you. Okay, I'll admit it. I used to like them, too.

Now take a break. Why don't you go grab a hot cup of tea? I know how you liked that. Bring it back with you. Tuck the afghan around you. Pretend I'm sitting right there beside you because in spirit I will be. And settle down for a trip down memory lane with me. Hurry. You know how I hate to wait.

Eve forced herself to stop reading as Bryan requested. Every cell in her body wanted to keep reading every single word and then re-read it over and over, again. But if Bryan had gone to all the trouble to write this letter and orchestrate her finding it, the least she could do was honor his wishes.

Her pulse skipped and her heart beat so fast it took her breath away. She remembered not all of their conversations were happy and light. She remembered the evening she asked him how he was coping. Bryan told her he wasn't afraid to die. He practiced his faith as he lived it, so it was no surprise to either of them that he found comfort in his faith as he died. He knew he was going to a better place. She was the one being left behind.

What touched her heart and simply amazed her was how he had been thinking of her and her feelings even during the very last weeks of his life. Planning ahead. Comforting her with little thought to what was happening to himself.

That was Bryan.

Her fingers gently traced the edges of the paper. His handwriting blurred as tears filled her eyes. She missed him so much. They'd had such a good life together, and then it was gone. She wondered if this heaviness in her heart would ever lift. She wondered if she'd ever be able to see a Christmas tree or hear a song or wrap a present without seeing images of Bryan in her mind. Then she wondered if she wanted to forget—ever—even if she could.

It was hard for her to put the letter down. Everything in her wanted to keep reading, keep hearing the sound of his voice in her head as her eyes flew across the words. But he'd put so much thought and planning into this unexpected gift that she didn't want to spoil it. Placing the letter on the table beside the sofa, she did as he requested and went into the kitchen to fix a cup of tea. She put a mug of water into the microwave and while it was heating, she rummaged through the cabinet looking for a bag of her Cinnamon Apple tea.

Eve glanced over at Pug. He'd gotten up from his nap, sat beside his bowl of food, and sniffed the air as if testing to see if there was anything more interesting than dog food nearby.

"Sorry, Pug. No pizza today. Or ham and turkey sandwiches. Eat your dog food." Eve chuckled. "I can't believe you jumped on that man's lap and stole his sandwich. What's the matter with you?"

The microwave beeped. She removed her mug, steeped her bag in the hot water, and took a second to enjoy the strong cinnamon aroma. She turned back and continued her conversation, no matter how one-sided, with the dog. "You're lucky Michael McGruder is a forgiving man, mister. Any other stranger may have picked you up and thrown you into traffic." The dog simply sat there staring at her.

"I have a surprise. I found a letter from Bryan, today. Isn't that wonderful?" She held a hand to her chest. "He's still with us, Pug. I know he is. I'll let you in on a little secret that I've never shared with anyone. Sometimes I think I catch a glimpse of him out of the corner of my eye, or I feel his warmth fold around me when I have a really bad day, or once in a while I swear I catch a whiff of his cologne."

Eve looked over at the dog and smiled. "You feel him, too, sometimes, don't you, Pug? You're not ready to let go, either." She lifted her mug, pushed away from the counter and headed toward the living room. "C'mon, boy. I'll read you the rest of Bryan's letter."

Eve settled down on the sofa, drew her feet up, covered herself with the afghan, leaned her head back and closed her eyes. She tried to picture Bryan hogging the blanket and dumping a bowl of popcorn in her lap right before they watched their movie.

I miss you. She sighed. *I miss us.*

She sat up and patted a place beside her on the sofa. Pug ignored her hand signal to join her, circled once or twice and found a spot in the doorway that satisfied him. Close but not too close. Eve wondered if the dog would ever warm up to her. As crazy as it seemed, sometimes she thought the dog actually blamed her for Bryan's death. She'd tried to think like Pug—that is if dogs had the ability to ponder things like human beings. All he knew was that one day she left with Bryan, who had been Pug's alpha dog and love of his life. They walked out the door without him. She was the only one who came back.

"Okay, Pug. I get it. It's all my fault." She sighed heavily. And maybe it was all her fault. Maybe the Universe had punished her because no human being should have ever been allowed to be that happy.

She sipped her tea, let the warmth spread through her, then picked up the letter and continued reading.

Let me guess. You're drinking Cinnamon Apple tea. The green tea comes out when you think you've gained a couple of pounds and you believe the media hype about it helping with weight loss. The regular black tea comes out when you're trying to focus or study and don't want coffee. And the Cinnamon Apple...that's the tea of choice for quiet evenings, relaxation, and movies.

See, Evie. I remember. I remember it all.

Do you remember the first day we met? I do. It was the Christmas season then, too. We were in kindergarten. My family had just moved to the area. It was my first day of school. I was scared and alone. Everyone else had already made friends. You were sitting at a table smearing green paint all over the palms of your hands. Then you pressed your hands onto a piece of paper. I was curious to see what you were doing. I ran over to your table but I tripped. My hands landed on top of yours and made you smear the Christmas trees you were making for your parents.

You were so mad. You yelled, stamped your foot, and started to cry. Even then, I couldn't bear to see you cry. You took one look at those splatted globs of paint that looked more like sausages than tree branches and you absolutely hated me. Even swatted at me with a green-stained hand until the teacher made you stop.

But I saved the day, didn't I?

I gave you the bag of M&M's packed in my lunch. The teacher helped you glue the candy to the branches like miniature Christmas balls. You ended up with the best-looking Christmas tree card in our whole class.

And our life-long friendship began.

We became active members of the BFF club long before we knew the first thing about computers or what those initials meant. But we were best friend forever, anyway. We played ball and rode bikes and fished in the pond and got into all kinds of mischief together.

As teens, we'd sneak phone calls to each other every night before we went to sleep. You commiserated with me through acne, a squeaky changing voice, and girlfriend problems. I listened to you as you struggled with your parent's constant arguments and, later, your dad's death.

We were friends. The best of friends. Until we weren't.

I'll never forget our junior prom. You had decided not to go even though I knew you'd received more than one invitation. Those years you were more tom boy than debutante and fancy clothes and dresses weren't your thing.

Becky Sullivan stood me up, one week before prom, choosing to accept a last minute invite from one of the football players, instead. Stereotypical, sure. I remember thinking I couldn't ever show my face in school again because everyone would know what had happened.

You were mad that she would hurt your friend like that. So you took your savings from working at the local pizza parlor, shopped all the thrift shops in town, and bought a gown. You showed up on my doorstep with a flower for my suit lapel, a corsage for yourself, and were determined to drag me to that prom to show Becky Sullivan just what she was missing.

That night changed everything, didn't it?

We danced every dance—first only the fast ones—and then, when Becky smirked one too many times, you dragged me onto the floor for a slow dance. Ah yes, that first wonderful slow dance. Awkward. Intense. Fantastic. Can you hear me chuckling? Can't help it. I'm remembering the slow dances that followed. We danced all night under that shimmering metallic silver ball. At first, we thought it'd be fun to pretend we were the real deal to make Becky and her date jealous. It was around slow dance number three when we both realized the only people we'd been fooling were ourselves. We were the real deal, and we were so much more to each other than friends.

From that day forward, through the rest of high school, college, marriage, good times, hard times, they all became our times.

Christmas belonged to us and the rest of the world simply shared it with us. From house to house carol singing, sled rides, church services, decorating our home inside and out. I proposed to you during the Christmas season, and the following Christmas you walked down a candlelit aisle and became my bride.

Then came the year I renamed you. Remember, that? I was so proud of myself making a play on words. You thought it corny, at first, but I thought it was great. One very special Christmas Eve you became my Christmas Evie. My beautiful, loving Christmas Evie.

Eve stopped reading. Tears misted her eyes and a myriad of emotions rushed through her. She wanted to go back in time and live their lives together all over again. She wanted to hear his voice not imagine it in her head. She wanted to stomp her foot and pretend getting angry when he'd pull his never-ending pranks, like the time he'd found a special gift she'd bought for him for one of his birthdays and hid it on her. He watched her tear the house apart looking for it. She was so mad when he revealed its hiding place and she realized what he'd done. He'd treated her to a memorable night on the town, a perfect dinner, and kissed all the anger away.

But this anger…

This anger was different.

She wanted to punch her hand through a wall. She wanted to scream at the top of her lungs. She wanted to sob until there wasn't a tear left in her body.

How dare he die!

She sobbed into her hands until her tears were spent and her anger subsided. She knew she was being ridiculous. What happened wasn't Bryan's fault. A shadow fell over her heart. But maybe that explained why she wasn't speaking to God as often anymore.

She clasped the letter to her chest as all those memories tumbled through her mind and took residence in her heart. She swiped away the wetness on her cheeks and tried to strengthen herself for the rest of the letter. Bryan loved her enough to give her this gift. She loved him enough to finish reading it although his words brought so much pain with them. She lowered the letter and resumed reading.

Remember how we loved taking evening walks down Main Street? The storefronts looked like they'd been flown in from the North Pole, decked out with bright lights, fake snow, glitter, and gifts galore. We'd look in the shop windows, often finding the perfect and unique gift for a family member or friend, and then laden with packages, smiles, and happy hearts, we'd buy hot soft pretzels and whipped creamed hot chocolate from the local vendors.

This was our Christmas past.

This year I want you to build new memories. New memories to pull out in years ahead and cherish.

After dinner, I want you to take a walk down Main Street. I want you to look in the shop windows, admire the lights, nod and say 'hi' to passing shoppers. I want you to buy a soft pretzel, maybe some hot cocoa from the local vendors.

Promise me, Evie. Promise me you'll do it.

When you do, I want you to smile and enjoy your holiday. I want you to be happy, Evie. I really do.

And know that for all our Christmases past, you were loved.

Bryan

Eve rested her head against the back of the sofa, closed her eyes, and clutched the letter to her chest for a long, long time.

Three

"What do you think, Michael? Do you think this tree is the right tree for me?" Dolores Sprocket, single, man-hungry Dolores Sprocket, had been chasing him for years, as well as every other single man she found out about. He'd made the mistake of going out for coffee with her once. He'd been trying to escape her clutches ever since.

"Dolores, how would I know if this was the right tree for you?" he asked, pasting a smile on his face and trying to hide his exasperation.

"Well, maybe we can put it on layaway. You can stop by my house tomorrow and take a look at the spot I have picked out for it and let me know what you think." She smiled up at him and accidentally-on-purpose leaned into him. "Come around five o'clock and I'll have a nice dinner prepared for you. As a thank you for your time, of course."

Was she batting her eyelashes?

Really?

Ouch. He'd walked into that one.

He inched back being sure not to dump her on the ground. "I'd love to help you, Delores, but as you can see," he said, waving his arm. "This is our busiest time of year. I can't saddle my dad with doing it all on his own." He placed his hands on her arms, steadied her, and took another step back. "Tell you what. Why don't you take another good look at the tree and try to picture it in that special spot you have picked out? If it feels right, I'll get it wrapped and tied to the top of your car right away. If not, you're welcome to spend time browsing. We have lots of other trees."

"I don't know…" Frown lines creased her forehead and she held an index finger against her lips.

Michael almost stumbled and fell as he moved farther away. "Take your time, Delores. You can let any one of us know when you decide what you want to do. I have to run."

He hurried across the lot and headed toward the checkout line.

Thank you, Lord, for small miracles, he prayed. *You know I don't want to hurt anyone's feelings. In Your infinite wisdom, and I know I'm speaking for many of the men here in Newton Falls, I'd be most grateful if You could find the right man for Delores and send him her way. We both know it's not me.*

Danny moved from behind the cash register. Laughing, he slapped his hand on Michael's back. "See you got yourself cornered over there."

"Some brother you are. I see you didn't bother to come over and help."

Danny continued to laugh and shrugged. "Thought you knew better."

"Where's Katie?" He glanced around and saw her standing next to her grandfather. "Never mind, I see her."

He started to move in her direction when Danny grabbed his arm. "Whoa, where are you going? We're slammed."

"We've been slammed and we're going to continue to be slammed. I need a break. I'm going to take Katie for a walk to see the lights and get her a soft pretzel. If I time it right, Dolores will be gone by the time I get back." He threw a glance over his shoulder. "If I were you, I'd send Dad over to help her. You're single, too, you know."

Danny laughed. "Yeah, but I'm pretty good at avoiding fishing nets. But sending Dad's a good idea. Ask him while you're over there." His brother waved him on.

"Hey, Dad. I think Dolores Sprocket might need some help." Michael nodded in the woman's direction as he clasped his daughter's hand. "I'm going to take a break for a bit."

"Where are we going, Daddy?" Katie asked as she skipped along beside him.

"We're going to take a walk up Main Street. I thought you might like to look in the shop windows and, maybe, if you're good, I'll buy you a soft pretzel."

"I'm always good, Daddy. You know that."

Michael smiled. "I can't argue with that, Katie." The tension in his shoulders instantly disappeared as he looked into his daughter's face. "Let's go have some fun."

"Hi, Mom. What's up?" Eve shifted the phone to her other ear while she fastened the leash onto Pug. "No, I'm not changing my mind. Because I don't want to spend Christmas in Florida." She led Pug into the garage and locked the back door behind her. "I know. I agree. Florida is a great place to visit, Mom. Yes, you can tell Connie I'll plan a trip there soon but not now."

She tethered Pug into the passenger seat of her Honda and then stepped around the car and slid into the driver's seat. "You know why, Mom. Please, stop worrying about me. I'm all right. I promise." She opened the garage door. "No, I am not sitting in the house all alone. I'm not. Matter of fact, I'm getting ready to hang up because Pug and I are in the car and we're going downtown to visit Main Street and maybe do some shopping."

She turned the key in the ignition. "Yes, I'm telling the truth. Can't you hear the car?" She held the phone away from her ear for a second and revved the engine. Then she put the phone back to her ear. "I know you and Connie are trying to make things better for me, Mom, and I appreciate it. I do. But Christmas in Florida isn't the way to do it. Not this year, anyway. I'm okay. Really. Yes, Mom. I'll talk to you tomorrow and tell you all about Main Street. Say hello to Connie. Good-night, Mom. I love you, too."

Eve shoved the phone in her pocket and backed out of the garage. She knew her mom and sister worried about her. Particularly with the anniversary of Bryan's death coming up the day after Christmas. But grief is something a person has to conquer on their own…with love and support and good wishes from friends and family, sure…but inevitably alone.

She asked herself more than once why she hadn't told either her mother or Connie about the letter she'd found last night from Bryan.

Maybe because she didn't want to subject herself to a million questions. But she knew that wasn't completely true. She got millions of questions from them every day, anyway, so this wouldn't be any different.

The reason went deeper.

The letter was—private.

A special, thoughtful, loving action by her dying husband to help her move through the grief. It was such a beautiful gesture, so intimate, so knowing and only between them. A gift she could cherish and read over and over again. An opportunity to hear Bryan's voice in her head almost as if he read the letter to her. She just couldn't share something so beautiful and intimate with anyone, not yet, maybe not ever.

She took a deep breath and continued driving toward town. The closer she got the higher her anxiety level soared. Her hands trembled slightly. Her breathing quickened. Her stomach felt like a boulder sized rock had taken up residence. She wasn't sure she could do what Bryan asked. Not yet. Not without him.

The sound of caroling wafted her way and the glow of twinkling lights caught her eye.

No. Not tonight. She needed to turn around before she got sick. This was hard. Too hard.

She didn't feel like walking down Main Street. She didn't want to look in shop windows or smile at people passing. She wanted to crawl under the afghan in the dark, sip wine, listen to sad music, and cry.

But…

If it had meant so much to Bryan that he took what little strength he had left to write the letter, then she'd honor his wish. She'd walk down Main Street if it killed her…and she'd smile…and she'd try with every pore in her body to find an ounce of holiday spirit still alive inside her heart.

She had to park her car two blocks away which was typical because Christmas on Main Street drew most of the town's residents each evening. All the shops went out of their way to decorate. The arbor held garland and lights overhead. Food vendors dotted the seven block stretch. Lanterns wrapped in red velvet ribbon lined the seven-block stretch until Main Street ended at the entrance to the town's park. There the highlight of the season would be a decorated gazebo with piped-in music resting at the lake's edge as both young and old glided across the frozen water on their skates.

Christmas on Main Street was always a festive time. The perfect place for a date night. Or family time. A time to have fun, sing songs, and build memories.

Eve forced herself to put one foot in front of the other and casually strolled down the street. She plastered a smile on her face. It didn't matter that the smile didn't reach her heart, did it? She nodded to each person she passed and even threw out a few 'hello's'.

Surprisingly, it didn't take long for the magic of the season to slowly seep into her heart. She hadn't gone more than two or three shops when she started seeing things she'd come back to buy for her family when she didn't have Pug with her. There was a cameo broach in the jeweler's window that was perfect for her mom. And she spotted a collection of pastel paints for her sister. She even found herself humming along with the passing Christmas carolers garbed in old-fashioned winter garb.

Her stomach growled, reminding her she hadn't had dinner. A cup of hot chocolate and a warmed soft pretzel sounded perfect just about now. Glancing up and down the street for the appropriate vendors, she almost missed the rattling motor rumble in the dog's chest. Almost. She tightened her hand on the leash and took a hurried glance around. Thankfully, the street was only open for foot traffic as he suddenly shot forward, nearly pulling her off of her feet as he dashed to the other side of the road.

"No, you don't!" Eve's eyes searched frantically for the poor soul who was about to be accosted by a food-stealing little thief. She yanked back on the leash but this dog took the set-back in stride and pulled harder, more determined than ever to reach the other side of the street.

"Ohhh, why can't you behave?" She yelled through clenched teeth as they threaded their way through other shoppers crossing the street in both directions.

Eve saw him almost at the same second he spotted her—Michael. Her gaze locked with those sapphire blue eyes seconds before he dropped his gaze to Pug. Hurriedly, he put his hands behind his back. Eve couldn't help but laugh. Obviously, the man had food and he wasn't about to be ambushed again.

"Pug!" A small, female voice called out and the little girl, arms open wide, embraced the dog the second they reached the sidewalk.

"Hello, again." Michael smiled at her. "I'd offer to shake your hand but my hands are too busy, at the moment, trying to hide our pretzels behind my back so your dog doesn't steal them."

Eve chuckled. "Good, idea. He's been behaving himself lately but I knew I was in trouble when he made his rumbling war cry and took off across the street." She glanced at the girl sitting on the ground, who giggled infectiously while getting her face licked over and over. "It looks like Pug was interested in something other than food this time." Eve tried another futile tug on the leash but the dog seemed as enamored with the girl as she was with him. "Your daughter's going to freeze sitting on that cold sidewalk."

"Don't worry, Katie is wearing two pair of leggings, pants and a long coat. She'll get up when she starts to feel cold." Michael brought his hands out from behind his back but still held them up high as an added caution from the food-napper. "Do you think it's safe or am I still a target?"

Eve shrugged. "I'm not sure. He hasn't bothered anybody else walking around with food tonight. I think you're safe. I guess he spotted your daughter and just wanted to say 'hello'." Eve looked around. "By the way, where did you buy them? I haven't seen the vendor anywhere."

"His cart is parked at the end of the street by the park." He offered her one of the two in his hand. "Here, you're welcome to take one of these."

She held up her palm. "Thanks, but no. I was just on my way to buy my own."

Michael glanced down at his daughter. "I think they're going to be busy playing for a little while. Katie, here's your pretzel." He leaned down, and with one suspicious eye on Pug, he gingerly handed it to his daughter.

Eve held her breath, praying Pug wouldn't grab it out of the girl's hand and take off. She gaped in disbelief when Pug sat down beside the child but didn't make any move to misbehave. In fact, the dog didn't move a muscle, and Eve wondered if it really was Pug or if someone had snuck in a clone.

Katie took a bite, licked her lips, and still Pug behaved. Eve smiled when Katie broke a small piece off and offered it to Pug who must have decided he wouldn't get in trouble for offered pretzels and he scarfed it up.

Michael chuckled. "Katie, only one or two tiny, tiny pieces. That dog doesn't need to get any fatter. It's not healthy for him."

"Okay, Daddy." She broke off a tiny little piece, put it in her palm and shoved it forward. He lapped the crumb and then again began covering her with wet dog kisses as Katie laughed.

"I've never seen Pug so enamored with a child before. He truly seems to like your daughter, and take it from me Pug doesn't like many people."

Michael grinned, his grin almost as breathtaking and mesmerizing as those beautiful blue eyes. "If we're smart we'll take advantage of the dog's distraction and enjoy this pretzel while it's still warm." Michael broke the remaining one in two and held out his hand. "If you won't take the whole thing, then at least accept half. I won't eat it in front of you and I'd love to take a bite while it's still hot."

"No, I can't."

He broke off a smaller piece. "Please. At least, take a bite. Then I won't feel guilty about eating in front of you."

"Only if you promise I can buy you another."

"Deal." He held out a piece and she took it.

"Ummm." Eve savored the first bite. "Nothing is better than a hot pretzel on a cold night."

"I agree." Michael took a bite of his own. When he finished chewing, he grinned. "So, what did your husband have to say about your flying dog fiasco?"

The blood drained from her face and the enjoyment of the moment disappeared like a vapor in the wind.

"What? Did I say something wrong?" Michael's concerned look blurred beneath the sudden moisture filling her eyes. "I'm sorry. I did, didn't I? I upset you. I'm so sorry."

Eve took a second to compose herself. She forced a smile and patted his forearm with her hand. "No. You didn't."

"But..."

She took a deep breath and said in a rush, "My husband died the day after Christmas last year. I...sometimes, I get overwhelmed with emotion."

"I'm sorry."

"It wasn't your fault. You didn't know." She tilted her head and sent him a puzzled look. "Did you know Bryan?"

He shook his head. "No. I never had the pleasure."

"Then how…?"

Michael nodded at the ring on her left hand. "I saw the ring and I assumed…" A deep frown pulled at his mouth. "Sorry."

She stared at the diamond sparkling beneath the holiday lights. She hadn't been able to take it off yet. She didn't know if she'd ever have the courage to. She shrugged. "How could you have known? Don't worry about it."

"Losing a spouse is never easy. But losing him the day after Christmas must make this holiday season a lot tougher. The first holiday after a loss is never easy."

Eve looked into his eyes. If she saw pity she would make an excuse, turn and walk away. She didn't want or need pity from anyone. But, instead, she saw empathy…and kindness…and concern.

"If there's anything I can do to help." He caught and held her gaze. "I know how hard it can be. I lost my wife shortly after Katie was born. I guess we're both members of a club neither one of us wanted to join."

"You lost your wife, too?" she asked, quietly.

He nodded.

She let the knowledge sink in for a moment. He was right. He did understand how she felt. They were members of a very cruel club, indeed. This was the second time she'd personally experienced how kind this man could be. When she smiled, this time it was genuine. "I know how you can help."

He arched an eyebrow and waited.

"Can I have another piece of that pretzel?"

Michael laughed and the sound eased the tension between them.

"Absolutely." He held out another healthy chunk and she took it. His fingers grazed hers. Frown lines creased his forehead and turned down the edges of his mouth. "Your hands are like ice. You should be wearing gloves." He reached into his pocket and pulled out a pair of work gloves. "These are ten times too big for you but you're welcome to wear them if you'd like."

"No, thanks, I'm fine." She tucked her hands into her coat pockets.

"Besides, shouldn't you be wearing them yourself?"

"I only wear them when I'm lifting and tying trees to people's cars."

So that's why she'd seen him sitting in a truck loaded with a bunch of pine trees.

"My family and I own McGruder Tree Farm about a twenty minute drive outside of town. We set up a sales lot every year across from the park for those who don't want to come out to the farm and cut down their own trees." Michael gestured over his shoulder. "Katie and I were just heading back. My brother and father are tending the place right now." He turned his attention to his daughter. "Katie, get up. We need to get back to help out Uncle Dan and Grandpop."

Katie bounced right up. "Can Pug come with us, Daddy? I want to show him all of our Christmas trees."

Michael shot a questioning glance Eve's way.

Eve noted the hopeful expression in the child's eyes and the way she bounced on the toes of her feet with anticipation. Eve smiled first at Katie and then at her father. "Since the vendor I'm looking for seems to be in the same direction, we'd be happy to walk with you."

"Can I hold the leash?" Katie stood in front of Eve with her hands folded together. "Please."

"Sure, if your dad says it's okay."

Michael nodded.

Eve looped the end of the leash around Katie's wrist as an extra safety measure, then let the child grab hold of the leash. "Be careful. Don't let him pull you. Remember you're walking him. He's not walking you."

Michael gave a hearty laugh. "If that's not the pot calling the kettle black. I saw you in a mad dash coming across the street." He lifted an eyebrow and a look of concern crossed his face. "Do you think my daughter can handle your dog?"

Eve couldn't help grinning. "I don't think Pug will pull on the leash if Katie is walking him. I truly believe he has a particular aversion to me and showers me with all his misbehaviors or I would never chance letting your daughter walk him."

Pug wagged his little stubby tail and licked Katie's hand.

"See?" Eve pointed. "The dog's in love."

Michael laughed. "Okay, we'll give it a try but I'm going to keep close to her just in case your dog gets any rebellious ideas so I can save my daughter from some skinned knees."

As Katie and Pug started walking down the street, she and Michael kept right on their heels. Once Michael seemed confident his daughter was safe, he seemed to relax. He shot a quick glance her way and smiled. "So I'm intrigued. What did you do to make this dog dislike you?"

"I outlived my husband."

The smile instantly disappeared from Michael's face.

"No, don't." Eve waved her hand at him. "I didn't mean to make you uncomfortable. What I should have said was Bryan was the alpha dog in our family and Pug adored him. Pug doesn't understand why Bryan doesn't come back and I have no way of explaining it to him. So he tolerates me and continues to wait for Bryan's return." She nodded at the pair. "That's the happiest I've seen Pug this entire year. He certainly likes Katie."

"He does, doesn't he? I guess he proved it when he didn't try to steal her pretzel." The grin was back on Michael's face.

Any anxiety Eve may have felt about allowing Katie to hold the leash disappeared because Pug seemed to be making an honest effort to be on his best behavior. He trotted beside Katie and didn't tug at all, seemingly intent on listening to every word Katie said as she acted as a tour guide and explained every place they passed.

Eve actually began to relax and enjoy her surroundings. The lights on the buildings, as well as those laced on the arbor above, were simply beautiful. Shoppers passed by laden with brightly colored shopping bags. A cold breeze carried the aroma of hot dogs and pretzels and cocoa on the evening air. It was turning out to be a lovely evening.

As their little group made their way to the end of the street, Michael chatted, sharing one story after another of prior year's Christmas tree disasters and other hysterical holiday stories. Eve hadn't laughed so hard in a long time—too long—and it felt good.

When they reached the tree lot, Michael's brother, Danny, recognized her. "Well, look who's here, the amazing flying dog and his owner." Danny grinned. "Good to see you again."

"Hi, Danny. Good to see you again, too." Eve glanced around the crowded lot. "Looks like business is good."

"Yep. It's been non-stop all night. Dad's running the cash register so I'm delegated to tree lifting and tying." He glanced over his shoulder. "Speaking of which, I better get back to it. Good to see you again, Eve, and if I don't see you beforehand, Merry Christmas."

"Thanks, Danny. You, too." Eve turned and noticed Michael was standing much closer than she'd thought. She literally bumped into his chest as she turned. She gazed up into his eyes and felt warmth flood her cheeks. Quickly, she moved away. "I should be going."

Michael pointed a finger over her shoulder. "There's the vendor you were looking for."

"I see him. Thanks." She started to reach for Pug's leash.

"Daddy can I walk with the lady and Pug a little longer. Please. Please."

Michael frowned and opened his mouth to speak but Eve interrupted before he could.

"That sounds like a wonderful idea. With your permission, I'll take Katie with me while I go pick up a couple of pretzels for all of us. It's just across the street and she seems to be doing a great job with Pug. She'll be in your sight the entire time."

Michael glanced at the vendor cart and then back to her. "If you're sure…"

Before he could finish, Katie was at Eve's side, Pug in tow. "Thanks, Daddy. See you later."

Eve laughed, clasped the child's hand and they started across the street. She chewed on her bottom lip.

What am I doing? I should have just said good-night and left.

She didn't want to examine her motivations too closely. She just knew that for the first time in a long time she was enjoying herself. She loved watching the interaction between Pug and Katie. And, she had to admit, she enjoyed Michael's company. He was kind and funny and not the slightest bit pushy. The fact that he'd lost his wife and knew how she felt made her feel like she'd found a friend, a kindred spirit, someone who wouldn't be watching her every move or weighing how heavy or how long her grief lasted like her mother and sister did. The fact that he was tall, dark and handsome had absolutely nothing to do with it. At least, that's what she told herself.

Eve purchased enough for all of them, including Danny and Sean.

The four adults gathered for a short break at the cash register table and ate the pretzels while they were warm. Katie didn't share any of hers with Pug this time and, surprisingly, Pug was fine with it.

If Eve didn't know better she would swear they were witnessing a Christmas miracle.

After they'd finished, Michael scooted his daughter, Pug and Eve in tow, toward an SUV parked only a few feet behind the cash register. Eve watched as Michael lifted Katie and placed her in a car seat in the backseat.

"I don't want to go home, daddy." Katie whined as she rubbed her tired eyes. "I want to play with Pug."

"It's late, Katie. Way past your bedtime. Maybe Mrs. Carlton will let Pug visit us another day."

Katie clapped her hands. "Can Pug come to visit again?"

Eve couldn't resist leaning in and pushing a strand of the child's hair off of her face. "Pug would love to come and visit you again, sometime. Now go home with your daddy and get some sleep. Walking Pug can make a person get pretty tired."

The child was already half asleep when Michael untied the leash from his daughter's wrist and handed it back to her. "Thanks, Eve, for letting her walk the dog."

"You're welcome. Obviously, Pug loved it."

Michael eyed the dog. "I must admit he's been on good behavior tonight. I'm surprised. I thought, for sure, my pretzels were goners."

"Me, too. Who knew?" She shrugged and chuckled.

Michael glanced down at his sleeping daughter. "She's been asking for a dog for almost as long as she could talk but the timing hasn't been right."

"Well, if Pug brought her a little joy, I think it's the least I could do after Pug's shenanigan's the other night."

Michael chuckled. "I'd say Pug made up for it nicely."

Eve smiled in return. "And thank you for sharing your food, the good conversation, and the company."

Michael's smile lit those sapphire eyes and crinkled his skin with laugh lines. "Anytime. I meant what I said. If there's anything I can do to make this season a little happier or your burden a little lighter, you know where to find me."

She nodded. "Thank you, but I'm fine."

He gave her a knowing look but remained silent.

She turned and waved good-bye to Michael's father, who gave an enthusiastic wave in return. Danny stopped for a second from tying a tree to the roof of a car and acknowledged her with his own wave and a friendly nod.

"You have a wonderful family." A sudden onset of shyness surprised her and she lowered her gaze.

Michael grinned. "Yeah, I think I'll keep them."

"Thanks, again," Eve said. "I had a pleasant evening."

He nodded and smiled into her eyes. "Anytime. I mean it."

With that, Eve turned and walked up the street toward her car. She'd had a pleasant night. Much better than she'd expected when she'd left the house. She'd have plenty to tell her mother during their phone conversation tomorrow. Good things.

But she couldn't stop the sudden moisture in her eyes or the lump that formed in her throat because the only person she really wanted to talk to about tonight was Bryan.

Michael silently watched Eve and Pug walk away. He wrestled with a mixture of emotions. He'd been surprised to see Eve again. More surprised to find out she was a recent widow. He'd meant it when he'd told her he knew how she felt. Even now, almost five years later, it didn't take much to bring memories of his deceased wife, Susan, to the surface. He'd taken a walk down memory lane himself the night Pug jumped onto his lap. He'd found himself thinking how much Susan would have enjoyed the story.

Michael knew pain fades but, thankfully, memories last. He had a million of them and was grateful for each and every one. Sometimes a certain way Katie tilted her head or smiled would remind him so much of her mother. Other times it could be something simple like eating at their favorite restaurant or just walking through the property at dusk and noting the sunset like they'd done so often. He smiled. Sometimes he'd even find himself talking to his wife and using her as a private sounding board when he had problems he was wrestling with. He knew she'd be with him always but, at least, the gut-wrenching grief was gone.

He was able to remember and talk about Susan with genuine affection and smiles. Good thing, too, since he saw Susan every time he looked into his daughter's face. But it had taken time, and tears, and prayers, and having the responsibility of caring for Katie when he could barely care for himself that eventually forced him to put one foot in front of the other and move forward.

He didn't envy Eve the difficult times ahead and offered up a silent prayer to the only one who could truly help her through it.

Four

Eve returned to Main Street several times over the next week. She'd avoided walking to the end of the street. Not because she had anything against Michael or his family. On the contrary, she liked the man. She found herself harboring feelings that confused her, and she just wasn't ready for any more confusion or pain. Besides, she'd already done her decorating when she'd pulled out the afghan. She didn't intend on putting up a tree so she had no reasonable explanation for ending up on their tree lot. She definitely didn't need the added calories of soft pretzels every evening, so she couldn't use the vendor as an excuse, either. So she'd glance down the street, smile at the memory of the pleasant evening they had shared, finish her shopping, and go home.

And shopping she did.

Although she'd already sent gifts to her mom, sister and sister's family, the Christmas spirit must be brewing because boy, oh boy, did she shop. She purchased not only the art kit she'd seen for her sister but a dozen brushes and some craft books. She bought the cameo for her mom and found an exquisite silk scarf she could wear with it. She bought a special fishing lure for her brother-in-law that she'd heard him speak about, and several toys for her nieces. She couldn't seem to help herself. She found something special in almost every shop she entered, including special treats for Pug.

And, of course, she took the Pastor's plea to fill a shoe box for needy children to heart.

She'd filled two.

Even Pug seemed to be feeling a little bit of Christmas spirit this year. He still kept his distance and did his best to ignore her. But she noticed that instead of hanging out in doorways, he'd started to inch his way a little closer to her each night, then would plop down and quietly watch her. He still refused to come closer if she called and he didn't like her to pet him. But he'd never settled down in the same room as her until lately. Hmmm.

Sunday morning Eve secured Pug out on the heated sun porch, filled his water dish, and warned him to behave. Then she hurried through the garage and slid behind the driver's side of her Honda Fit.

She'd been attending this particular bible-based church for the past fifteen years. Matter of fact, the pastor had married them. And the pastor had set-up grief counseling sessions for her right after Bryan's death. It was a growing church, active in the community, and last count had a membership of almost two thousand people. Yet, it felt small. It felt like family. It felt like home.

Now, juggling the two boxes in her arms that she'd packed for needy children, she made her way across the church foyer to the far table set up to collect the boxes. Afraid she was late, she wasn't paying attention to the people around her as she brushed past them. She almost stumbled when a little child ran up beside her and tugged on her dress.

"Hi, Miss Eve. Remember me? It's Katie."

Eve came to an abrupt halt and looked down at the face smiling up at her. As if she could ever forget that angelic face dusted with freckles or her ebony hair braided into pig tails.

"Hi, Katie. I didn't know you came to this church, too." Eve glanced up looking for Michael and saw the Sean McGruder approaching quickly, instead. The concerned look on his face, as well as the woman by his side, gave Eve pause.

"Katie, what did I tell you?" Sean scolded as he reached them. "You are never, ever supposed to run off. You must always stay with me or your grandmother. Understand?" Then he glanced at Eve. "I'm sorry, Eve. I hope this little one hasn't been bothering you." He frowned at the child again. "She knows better than to run off by herself."

"Sorry, Grandpop, but I saw Miss Eve and I wanted to say hello." The child looked back and forth. "Did you bring Pug to church, too?"

"No, honey. Pug stayed home today."

Eve crouched down so she was eye-level with the girl. "Katie, your grandfather is right. There are lots and lots of people that come to this church. You are little and you could get lost if you go off by yourself.

Besides," she winked and smiled. "I don't know about you but I sure don't want to be on Santa's naughty list this close to Christmas."

Katie's eyes widened and her mouth formed a perfect little circle. She reached over and grabbed her grandfather's hand. "I'm sorry, Grandpop. I won't do it again. I promise."

Sean shot Eve a grin but kept his tone of voice stern. "You better not, young lady."

A well-dressed, pleasant looking woman standing beside Sean wagged her index finger at the girl. "If you run off like that again, young lady, you are going to lose your TV privileges for an entire week. Do you understand? You scared us. We didn't see where you went and we thought we lost you."

"I'm sorry. I just wanted to say 'hi' to Ms. Eve and see if she brought Pug to church, too. I won't do it again. Please don't tell Santa."

The older woman stifled a smile. "Well, I'll forgive you just this once, but if you try and run off again I will sit down and write a letter to Santa myself. Understood?"

The child, looking completely remorseful, leaned against her grandfather's leg and nodded.

The woman looked over at Eve and grinned. "Hello. I'm Ruth McGruder. From the sounds of it, you must be the owner of the infamous flying dog. I would have loved to be there to see it."

Eve smiled. "I'm Eve. Nice to meet you. I'm responsible for Pug, but I can't claim to own him. Pug is a tenacious creature who picks and chooses who owns him. I think I'm still on his to-be-determined list, but the dog seems to have taken a shine to Katie."

Ruth patted the child's hair. "So I've heard."

Eve couldn't help taking a quick glance around the foyer looking for Michael but she didn't see him. "Well, nice to meet you but, if you'll excuse me, I need to drop these shoeboxes off at the collection table."

Katie chimed in. "That's where we're meeting daddy," Katie chimed in. "Want to come with us?"

Eve chuckled at the child's enthusiasm and tried to ignore the little skip in her pulse at the thought of seeing Michael again. "Sure." The four of them moved as a group toward the other side of the church foyer.

Eve spotted him seconds before he saw her. When he did, he smiled, not a polite smile he seemed to offer everyone approaching the table, but what looked like a genuine, he-looks-happy-to-see-me smile, which caused her pulse to skip, again, followed by a twinge of guilt that she should be so happy to see him.

"Eve." He stood and lifted the boxes from her hands. "I didn't know you attended this church. Good to see you."

"I didn't know you attended here, either. But with over two thousand members, it doesn't surprise me that we haven't run into each other before."

"Daddy are you done? Can we go now? Please." Katie bounced on the balls of her feet, obviously excited about something.

"Katie, don't interrupt when Daddy is talking. It isn't polite." Michael corrected his daughter and then turned his attention back to Eve. "I promised her I'd take her skating at the park and I guess she's a little excited."

"Skating?" Eve smiled down at the child. "That sounds like oodles and oodles of fun. No wonder you're excited. It's a perfect day to be out on the lake."

"Do you skate?" Ruth asked. "You're welcome to join us."

"Absolutely," Michael seconded. "We'd love to have you join us."

"I appreciate the offer, Mrs. McGruder…"

"Call me Ruth. I might be a grandmother but I'm not ancient yet."

Eve chuckled. "Ruth. I appreciate the offer. I do. But I've never learned how to skate."

"You don't know how to skate? Really? I thought every kid learned how to skate when they're little," Sean said. He huffed out a breath when his wife jabbed her elbow into his side. "What? Why'd you do that?"

Eve chuckled. "You're right. Most kids learn to skate when they're little. It's something I've always wanted to do, but, for one reason or another, the opportunity never presented itself."

Katie grabbed her hand and jumped up and down. "We'll teach you Miss Eve. My daddy and my Uncle Danny teach me. Daddy is a good teacher. He can teach you. Can't you, Daddy?"

A warm tell-tale flush crept up Eve's neck and, knowing her cheeks would soon be beet red, she couldn't make eye contact with Michael.

His gravelly chuckle felt like a warm caress to her nerve endings and only made matters worse. "I'd be happy to teach you to skate, Eve. What do you say? Will you join us? It should be fun."

Eve's heart raced and she could, literally, feel her pulse pound in her throat. She'd always wanted to learn to skate and now the opportunity was right in front of her. She thought back to Bryan's letter, encouraging her to try new things and build new memories. Skating would definitely be building a new memory.

But being taught by Michael?

She wasn't sure that was such a good idea. She was strongly attracted to him. She didn't understand it. She definitely didn't want it. But she was. And it made her uncomfortable and confused.

Ruth placed a hand on Eve's forearm. "We'd love to have you join us, dear." The compassion she saw in the older woman's eyes made her realize Michael must have told them not just about Pug's misadventures, but also about Bryan's death. She hesitated for just an instant, and then, as if some inner force she couldn't control gave her a giant push, she smiled at the four people staring at her as they waited for her answer.

"I'd love to. But I'll have to meet you there. I need to stop at the house and change my clothes." She glanced down at her dress and high heels. "I have a feeling I need to wear something warm since I will probably be spending a lot of time sitting on the ice."

The sound of this family's laughter and the smile on their faces warmed Eve's heart more than they could ever know.

Michael finished lacing Katie's skates. When his daughter stood up and started to hop in place, he reached out and steadied her to prevent her from falling. "Katie, stop! You're going to fall before you even hit the ice."

"Look, Daddy!" His daughter pointed over his shoulder. "Ms. Eve is here and Pug is here, too."

Michael straightened from his crouched position. His heart pounded a new rhythm at the mere sight of Eve making her way from the parking lot towards them. His lips twisted into a frown. *What's wrong with me? I'm reacting like a foolish teenager with a crush.*

He didn't know why this woman affected him the way she did. Sure, she was attractive. But he'd met many attractive women over the years, even hooked up a few times with one or two over the years, yet none of them made his pulse skip or a warmth run through his body like she did. And, yes, he'd had a really good time with her last week on Main Street. But this wasn't physical lust. He recognized that stuff. This was something more, a deeper attraction that he hadn't felt for anyone since his wife.

Maybe that's it. They had bonded over the shared loss of their spouses, connecting them with an understanding and empathy few others understood.

Yeah, that's what it is.

Sure.

Eve's smile broadened as she came closer and he swore his heart did a somersault in his chest.

Heck, no. Empathy doesn't surge testosterone to 100% of his male anatomy.

His frown quickly changed to match her wide grin while he struggled to manage any physical reaction. He nodded toward Pug as the dog made a beeline for Katie. "I see you brought Pug. Does he need skating lessons, too?"

She chuckled at his teasing. "I've chickened out on the lessons. But I thought I'd still like to watch and, of course, Pug always enjoys a walk in the park."

Michael's parents and Danny walked over and greeted her.

"Why are you chickening out on skating lessons?" Michael asked.

"Chickening out?" Danny raised an eyebrow. "Are you sure? I don't compliment my brother often, but I promise he is an excellent skater. If anyone can show you the ropes, he can."

Michael loved the way she dropped her gaze and a perfect shade of pink slowly slid up her throat and tinged her cheeks. Could it be he wasn't the only one feeling a bit adolescent right about now?

"I don't have any skates," she said with a shrug.

"No, problem." Sean McGruder gestured over his shoulder. "There's a skate rental set up next to the gazebo."

Eve glanced toward the gazebo but she still looked hesitant.

"C'mon, Ms. Eve, it'll be fun." Katie reached over and tugged at her hand.

"But Pug…"

"Don't worry, dear. We'll watch the dog," Ruth grinned, obviously removing her last excuse.

Michael stepped closer and caught her gaze. "Looks like you're outvoted. You never should have told this crew that you wanted to learn to skate. They won't give up, now." He gently cupped her elbow in his palm and offered his most charming smile. "What do you say? Feel like having a little bit of fun?"

A multitude of emotions flashed across her face as she struggled with making a decision. Michael knew it wasn't a decision about a skating lesson, at all. She seemed to be as attracted to him as he was to her and it bothered her. Maybe even scared her a little. A year can seem like an eternity when grieving, and yet not long enough when real life starts pulling you out of that hole. He smiled. And he waited. He wasn't aware he'd been holding his breath until she smiled.

"Sure," she whispered. "Why not?"

"Yay!" Katie clapped her gloved hands together. She hopped, slid, and Uncle Danny caught her under her arms before she fell. "Whoa, Katie. You're going to fall enough times on the ice. Let's try not to fall on dry land."

Everyone chuckled as Danny gently steered the girl toward the ice. Ruth stepped closer and, taking Pug's leash from Eve's hand, placed another light touch on Michael's sleeve and shot him a warm, knowing glance only mothers can do. "Go on, you two. Have fun. Danny is taking care of Katie. We'll take Pug for a walk and then meet both of you under the gazebo when you're finished Katie's skating lesson."

Katie looked a little bewildered as the family that had instantly appeared, just as quickly disappeared, leaving just the two of them standing together at the edge of the pond.

"You're going to have fun," he promised. "Trust me." He tucked his hand beneath her elbow. "C'mon. Let's get you some skates."

She didn't pull her arm away as they made their way to the rental booth. That's a good sign, right? Don't push it McGruder. Take it slow. Real slow.

Once they'd gotten her skates, he led her back to the gazebo. She sat and leaned over to don the skates. When she finished, Michael crouched down to double check her lacing and make sure it was tight enough to offer her ankles firm enough support. Standing up, he held out his hand, and grinned. "Lesson number one. Walk very gingerly. Skates work much better on ice then on dry land."

Her hand felt tiny and her fingers soft against his weather-worn skin. "Don't tell me you forgot to wear gloves again?"

She shook her head, reached into her coat pocket, and retrieved a pair.

"Good thing," he said.

She slid them on, then he clasped her elbow and helped her onto the ice.

He almost laughed out loud at the look of surprise on her face as, for the first time, she felt her blades glide her a foot or two on the ice. Her eyes widened and she did the typical windmill arm waving and swaying as she tried to keep her balance. She slid to a stop and just froze, almost as if she was afraid to move a muscle. The expression on her face was one of terror but the look in her eyes was pure exhilaration.

"It's okay. Relax. Take a deep breath. I'm right here." Michael slid an arm around her waist and pulled her close. He felt rather than heard her inhale deeply and her body stiffen. "Don't worry. I won't let you fall. Just listen to my voice, do what I say, and most of all, try to relax. Enjoy yourself. This is supposed to be fun, remember?"

She nodded her understanding but her eyes still looked like a deer caught in headlights.

With a wide grin, he nodded and said, "Good. Now, slowly slide your right foot forward and once to you start glide, move your left foot forward the same way, and then repeat the process."

Excitement shone in her eyes followed by a flash of hesitation.

"I must be crazy." She clenched his hand in a death grip. "I'm not a child, anymore. If I fall, I could seriously break a hip or something."

"Don't worry," he whispered next to her ear. "It'll be okay. I've got this."

She looked into his eyes. Her body relaxed beneath his hands and that small offer of trust was enough to stir his desire to protect her. He intended to do his best to teach this woman to skate and, if he was lucky, she might even enjoy the chance to achieve a childhood dream. But either way, he knew one thing for certain. Under no circumstances, no matter what, was he going to let her fall.

"Ready?" he asked.

She smiled and offered a slight nod.

They pushed off together, slowly gliding first to the right and then to the left. He held her tightly against his side using his body and his arm to steer her and make her feel secure. They'd barely made it a dozen yards when her timidity eased. Her smile couldn't have stretched any wider. A bubble of nervous laughter continually filled the air but her eyes—her eyes told it all—they were lit with the glee of a child on Christmas morning.

Michael taught her how to stop, how to turn, even released his hold on her waist and moved to her side, holding her hand as they slowly and carefully started to glide across the pond in unison. Danny and Katie appeared, stumbling and gliding right alongside them. Laughter and hoots and hollers of encouragement filled the air as the four of them skated together. Michael thought his face would crack from grinning. He'd remember this day for a long time and hoped Eve would, too. This day was one of those special days that come along and seem perfect. Simply perfect.

Five

Katie leaned heavily on the arm of Michael's chair. "Can we go ice skating again, Daddy?"

"Sure." Michael, trying to finish the paperwork for his latest shipment of trees, answered without even glancing up at his daughter.

"Today?" she pleaded.

"Huh?" He replied, still not looking up.

"Daddy!" Katie stamped her foot. "You're not listening to me."

Okay, that caught my attention.

He chuckled, pushed the paperwork to the side, and looked up.

"I want to go skating, today, Daddy" Katie insisted, when she saw she had his attention.

"Sorry, honey. No can do. Uncle Danny and I have appointments this afternoon to take people up the trail to pick out their Christmas trees. We want to make sure everybody gets a tree in time for Christmas, don't we?"

Her perfect little mouth twisted in a crooked grimace as she thought about his question. "Oh-kay." She hung on the chair arm, bent her knees, and held her feet in the air. "Can we go after the people get their tree?"

"Not today. Maybe I'll take you again this weekend."

"It was so-o-o-o much fun, wasn't it, Daddy?"

Michael smiled at his daughter. "It was bunches and bunches of fun."

"And I only fell down this many times." Katie lifted her hands to count on her fingers, forgetting her feet were off the ground. She plopped in a heap on the floor.

Michael jumped up and leaned over to help her up. "You, okay?"

Katie nodded vigorously. Then she held up her fingers. "I only fell this many times." She scrambled to her feet. "And Ms. Eve didn't fall even one time. You caught her every time, didn't you, Daddy?"

Michael nodded. "Yep, I guess I did."

"I don't know why Miss. Eve was so scared about falling. I fall all the time. Uncle Danny caught me a lot but I still fell when he wasn't looking. It doesn't hurt. But I'm glad you caught Miss. Eve. I didn't want her to fall." When he sat back down, she climbed onto his lap. "Do you think we can ask Miss. Eve to come skating with us, again? And we'll tell her to bring Pug with her. He looked so funny when he tried to walk on the ice. He slipped and slid all over the place and he didn't even have skates on. Wasn't he funny?"

Michael laughed. "You're right. Watching him try to walk on ice was almost as funny as seeing the dog fly through the air when he stole my sandwich."

Katie clapped her hands together. "Do you think Miss Eve and Pug will come? I really want them to come with us."

"I don't know, honey. This is a very busy time of year and Ms. Eve is probably pretty busy."

Busy enough not to return any of my calls.

"You need to ask her, Daddy. Please."

"I will, Pumpkin. But don't be disappointed if she can't make it."

She snuggled closer in his arms. "I want her to come with us, Daddy. I want to see, Pug, too."

"I know. I do, too. Maybe if she can't go skating with us, we can get her to visit us here."

"I can show Pug all our trees."

"That would be great, honey."

I hope Katie isn't too disappointed, if she says no. Heck, I hope I'm not disappointed. He smiled to himself. *I'll just have to make sure that I make her an offer she can't refuse.*

He snuggled with his daughter and allowed his thoughts to plan a way for all of them to see Eve and Pug again—soon.

49

"Hi, Mom. Yes, I'm fine. How's everything there?" Eve held her cell phone between her face and shoulder and carried her cup of black tea over to the table. She had a million things to do today and she needed the boost. "Yes, I'm sure Disney is beautiful this time of year." She plopped down in a chair, adjusted the phone, and stirred her tea. "Uh-huh. Sounds beautiful."

Eve squeezed her eyes shut and crinkled her mouth when the inevitable questions came her way. "Yes, Mom, I already told you I had a great time skating. Of course, I will go again. When? I don't know. Someday." She sighed. "I agree. It was very nice of Michael's family to include me in their Sunday outing. Mom, please, don't try to make more of it than it was." She listened for a few more seconds and then said, "Look, Mom, I have to run." She held the phone away from her ear. "I'm losing you, Mom. The connection is acting up." She couldn't believe she was actually trying to make static noises with her mouth. "Bye, Mom. Luv, ya."

She tossed the phone on the table, sat back in her chair, and stared at the kitchen ceiling.

No question her mother loved her, but her continual questions made Eve want to duck the calls not take them. You can't push a person through grief. And, sometimes, her mom made her feel like she wasn't moving forward fast enough.

Maybe the problem wasn't that she was moving too slowly. Maybe the real problem was she might be moving too fast. Skating the other day had been so much fun. Exciting. Exhilarating. Everything she'd ever thought it could be. Cold air kissing her cheeks and blowing her hair as she glided almost weightlessly across the ice.

Michael's family are welcoming and fun. His daughter is too cute for words. And Michael...

The heat of his breath on her neck had caused chills to dance along her skin. She had leaned so naturally into the strength of his arms as he tucked her against his body. They moved across the ice in flawless rhythm, two bodies moving in tune, both physically and emotionally. And it was awesome.

Pug sat at the edge of the kitchen doorway and stared at her.

"What?" She couldn't keep exasperation out of her voice.

The dog continued to sit and stare. Little fingers of guilt climbed up her spine as she stared right back.

"I know, Pug. I get it. You think I should be as miserable as you." She sighed deeply. "And I am! I swear, Pug, I would do anything, if I could bring Bryan back. I can't!" Her words escaped in an agonized whisper. "I can't."

"Don't sit there judging me." She frowned at the dog. "If I remember correctly, you were having a pretty good time with those McGruders, too." She wagged a finger at him. "It's the timing. It couldn't be worse. Don't you think I get that? I'm not supposed to be attracted to any man right now. I'm not supposed to laugh or have fun. I know, Pug! You don't have to stare me down to remind me. I've been saying the same thing to myself for the past four days."

She got up and walked into the den, Pug on her heels, close but not too close.

"Do you think I want to sit around thinking about Michael? I don't. I don't want to dwell on his kindness, or the deep richness of his voice, or the scent of fir trees and his own male scent on his skin. I don't want to enjoy counting the laugh lines crinkling his skin or drown in those deep, rich blue eyes or share soft pretzels and laughs. I don't want to think about how much I've enjoyed every minute of each time I've been with the man. I swear I don't, Pug." She cupped her face in her hands and leaned her elbows on her knees. "But I do."

She thought back to Bryan's letter. He wanted her to be happy. He'd said so several times. So where was all this guilt coming from? Bryan was right. She had to move on.

Pug cocked his head and studied her but otherwise didn't move.

"What am I going to do, Pug? I've purposely avoided Main Street all week so I couldn't run into Michael or any of his family. I haven't returned the two voicemails he left on my phone even though I thought it was sweet of him to check up on me and see how I was doing."

She patted a place on the sofa beside her but Pug ignored her. She sighed and ignored him. "Fine, be that way. But stop staring at me. I can't just hole up in this house for the rest of December and not see anyone or talk to anyone or do anything. That's not healthy. Besides, Bryan wouldn't want that for me. He said so in his letter. He encouraged me to go out. He wants me to see the sights and enjoy the holiday." She leaned over and tried to pet the dog but Pug immediately moved out of reach.

"Okay, fine. Punish me. I deserve it. But don't think these confusing thoughts I'm having about Michael takes away any of the pain I feel about losing Bryan. I loved him, too, you silly, food-stealing dog! I loved him with all my heart." Her eyes stung with the tears threatening to spill down her cheeks. "But he left us, Pug. I know he didn't want to but he's gone. And I don't know what to do with all of this loneliness and pain."

It was probably her imagination but she could have sworn Pug moved closer to her on purpose. Not close enough for her to pet him but close enough to maybe offer a crumb of empathy.

Boy, I am really losing it if I think this crazy dog can understand me...or care.

"Well, I know what I'm going to do. I'm going to pull out the Christmas decorations. I know I said that wasn't on the agenda, but I feel strongly that Bryan would want me to do it. After all, he tucked his letter into Grandma's Christmas afghan. He sent me shopping on Main Street. He's probably expecting me to decorate for the holidays. He wants me to be happy this holiday season, Pug. And he wants you to be happy, too, boy."

She rubbed her hands together and clamped her teeth shut with renewed determination.

"So that's what we're going to do, Pug. We're going to pull out the decorations and bring some holiday spirit into this house. We're going buy a tree, hang lights, string garland, and put a wreath on the front door. Bryan will be so proud of us."

Eve fisted her hands on her hips, and grinned at the dog lying in the doorway. "You know what? I'm going to pull out all of your Christmas sweaters. Bryan loved dressing you up. He treated you like a live doll, and you can't tell me you didn't like all of the extra attention. I'm even going to rummage through the attic until I find those ridiculous reindeer ears. Yes, Pug, you *are* going to wear those ears. We are going to celebrate Bryan's life, not cry over it. We're going to make this one of the best Christmases we can and we're going to do it in memory of Bryan. Because we love him. Both of us. C'mon. Let's go look for those ears."

Making multiple trips back and forth from the attic, Eve covered the spread on her bed with boxes of holiday decorations filled with garlands, glitter, ornaments, and everything Christmas. She held her breath waiting for that familiar pang of guilt to wash over her—but it didn't. Satisfaction, even a glimmer of happiness, made her smile.

She removed the lid from one of the boxes closest to her and laughed out loud. This box held their entire collection of ugly Christmas sweaters. Reaching inside the box, she pulled out a set of reindeer ears. "Aha! Look, I didn't even have to search for it." She waved the ears in the air, showing them to the dog lying in the bedroom doorway and laughed. "You're going to look so cute!"

Placing the ears back on the bed, she lifted the lid off a second box, then paused. She smiled as she saw the contents. Her fingertips gently caressed the two top ornaments. One was a miniature rocking horse and the other was a Christmas baby angel. She even remembered when and where they'd purchased them. They purchased the angel on a day trip to Manhattan and they found the hand-carved rocking horse in an adorable little Amish wood-working shop in Lancaster County.

Eve gently probed through the rest of the contents of the box. Each ornament represented so much more than a mere Christmas ornament. They were the result of trips, movies, or something unusual that held heartfelt meaning special only to them. This box held memories of a marriage filled with happiness and expectations.

They'd been so young and so very much in love. They'd believed they had an entire lifetime of equally great times stretching before them. She wondered if they would have done anything differently if they'd known how precious few weekends like that they had left.

No. You're not going to let memories bring you down. Not today.

Instead, she wrapped her memories around her like a comforting, warm blanket on a cold, winter night. It felt good to reflect back on their life together. They'd had a good life, every day filled with conversations, hard work, laughter, love, petty arguments always followed with great make-up sex. She could honestly say she had no regrets. They'd been content, happy. How many people could say that about their lives?

For the first time in many months, Eve's thoughts didn't cause tears but brought actual smiles. Sure, she hated the idea that life kept going one day after another whether Bryan was still here or not. She hated the fact that she had to learn to move forward with a life without Bryan in it. He had died so young and that would never be okay.

But they'd had kindergarten, middle school, high school, college, marriage. A mini lifetime together. She needed to cherish that fact and count her blessings.

Eve's eye caught the edge of something poking out from beneath one of the ornaments. She grabbed the edge with her fingernails and, slowly, slid it out.

A second letter from Bryan.

Of course.

 Six

Eve's smile stretched into a full-fledged grin. Bryan did it again. He left her another piece of his heart. Half of her wanted to rip open the envelope as quickly as possible to see what treasures it held. Her other half wanted to savor the moment, stare at the familiar handwriting, appreciate the time and planning Bryan had put into providing this surprise.

Pug must have sensed something. The silly dog belly-crawled from the open doorway and came to a stop merely an arm's length away. Then, he sat up, cocked his head, and stared at her.

Eve laughed out loud. "Careful, Pug. You're getting pretty close to me. You don't want to break your record of being aloof and indifferent, do you? Some people might think you're starting to like me."

Pug whined.

Eve grinned. "What? This?" She held up the letter for Pug to see. "How do you know it's from Bryan?" She waved it in the air. "You do know, though, don't you?"

Pug wagged his tail and whined louder.

"Okay. Be quiet. I'll read it." She slid her fingernail under the sealed flap and pulled out the letter. Her eyes misted and all she could see was a blur of ink. She squeezed her eyes shut and took a slow, deep breath. She couldn't believe Bryan had left her not one but two letters. But that was Bryan, thoughtful and always conjuring up surprises for her.

Ohhh, Bryan. I miss you so much.

Pug whined again. The dog got up, turned in a circle, sat back down, and resumed staring at her.

Eve chuckled. "Okay, Pug. You'd think the letter was written to you, you silly dog." She unfolded the pages and began to read aloud.

Hi honey,

Me, again. Bet you didn't think you'd get a second letter, huh? What can I tell you? You know me. I'm the King of Surprises.

Seriously, though, I'm thrilled you found this letter. It means you've pulled the Christmas decorations out. Hurray, honey! I can't tell you how happy it makes me to know that you are decorating the house for the holiday, that you are moving forward with your life, that you're building new memories.

No, don't say it. Don't even think it. No guilt, understand? And that's exactly what you're doing, isn't it? You're letting every happy thought or experience this holiday season become tainted because you don't believe you should be happy without me. I know you pretty well, don't I?

Well, you know me, too. You know exactly what I'm going to say. That your crazy self-talk is just stinkin' thinkin', so knock it off. I want you to be happy, Eve, always, but particularly at this time of year, particularly now when you're navigating these new waters without me and you think you're all alone.

But you're not.

Close your eyes, Evie. Take a deep breath. Don't move. Don't breathe. Just let yourself feel.

Can you feel the warmth of my arms holding you tight? Can you hear the sound of my voice in your head as you read these words?

I'm here—for as long as you need me.

Request number one: I want you to smile and shoo any unhappy thoughts away.

Easy, right?

Okay, maybe not so easy but something I want you to do anyway.

I hope you did the things I requested in my last letter. I hope you took just a few moments to reflect on all our Christmas's past and that those memories made you happy.

We had so many great times, didn't we?

But then I hope you got up, got out, and got going. I hope you shopped on Main Street and ate soft pretzels and drank hot chocolate and maybe even sang a song or two in your adorable off-key way. Sorry, Evie, but I have to be truthful. You're perfect in so many ways but you can't carry a tune to save your life. Remember you sang at my company summer picnic? Every dog within miles howled.

But back to Main Street. I hope you said hello to passerby's and maybe even made a new friend or two. I hope you had fun and started building new memories.

The past is past, Evie, and that's where it belongs. It's nice to reflect on it, pull out a memory or two, and then tuck them away where they belong, in the past.

So let's talk about the now. Today. Living today, this Christmas.

I'm picturing you sitting among boxes of ornaments and all our other house decorations. This is exactly where I want you to be. Getting ready to celebrate our favorite holiday. Getting ready to bring light and happiness to a house I know has been too dark this past year. It would break my heart to think you're pining away for things that are gone and can't be brought back. One of us with a broken heart is one too many, don't you think?

So pay attention, love. These are the things I want you to do this year...for me...for us.

Request number two: I want you to drive out to McGruder's Tree Farm and pick out the biggest, best tree you can find. Do you remember Mr. McGruder? He was such a nice older man. He never rushed us. He showed the patience of a saint. You had the hardest time choosing our tree. One had perfect branches but wasn't tall enough. Another had a bare spot in the back. Another was gorgeous but too tall. So you'd flit and you'd wander. Mr. McGruder and I joked that you looked at every single tree on his entire farm. Just when we'd decided you would never be able to choose and we'd have to do it for you, you'd choose. And the nice old guy always assured us we'd picked the best one.

McGruder? Could it be? She couldn't remember ever seeing or meeting Michael McGruder before, or his brother, Danny. She vaguely remembered an older man walking with them through the woods while they shopped. Maybe because Bryan was the one who had lagged behind and carried on a conversation with the gentleman as she raced ahead from tree to tree. She'd done little more than offer the older man a 'hello', a nod of her head, and friendly smile.

Could that really have been Michael's father? No way!

But, of course, it had to be them. It all made sense now. They were driving a truck full of Christmas trees. They had a tree lot on the edge of Main Street and mentioned they had a tree farm. It couldn't be anyone else. Coincidences like this didn't just happen, did they?

A chill raced up and down her arms and she shivered. How odd that out of all the cars and trucks Pug could have chosen to jump into, he chose theirs. Still reeling from the coincidences, she picked up the letter and read.

I want you to carry on our tradition, Evie. Pick the tallest, fattest, prettiest tree you've ever seen. I bet if you tell Mr. McGruder why I'm not with you this year and ask if, for an extra fee, he could possibly deliver the tree and set it up for you, he will.

Just in case he doesn't have the time, since this is his busy season, ask our neighbor, Stan. I spoke to him last year when I was getting ready to write these letters and he promised he'd help you put up the tree if you asked him.

Eve smiled. Now she understood why Stan had stopped by twice in the last two weeks, supposedly just to say hello, see how she was doing, and wish her a happy holiday. Poor Stan. He was a great guy. Always there to help but never poking his nose into other people's business. The perfect neighbor. Trying to honor Bryan's request without coming out and asking her if she was going to put up a tree this year. She'd offered him a tray of cookies to take home to his wife and pondered why he kept showing up. She'd have to put him out of his misery next time she saw him and let him know Bryan had told her about the arrangement. She shook her head. My dear, sweet Bryan, you thought of everything didn't you?

Pug scooted a couple of inches closer and let out a soft whine.

"Okay. Hold on." Amazing how the dog seemed to know the letter was from Bryan. Intelligently, she knew that wasn't possible but one look at that dog's rapt attention and wagging tail told her heart another story.

She glanced at the paper clutched in her hands. Sometimes a particularly moving or exciting book made her wish the story wouldn't end.

That's how she felt now. She didn't want this letter to end. She wanted to keep reading Bryan's words, keep hearing his voice in her mind and...

And never, ever wanted to say good-bye.

But her eyes strayed to the page, anyway.

As I'm writing this letter, I'm picturing how beautiful your tree is going to look, covered with each and every one of our "special" ornaments. I'm remembering each trip, every reason known only to us for choosing each ornament—like the year we took a trip to San Francisco and we found a holiday decorated trolley car. Or the year we found a pug dog wearing a Santa Claus hat. It would have been funnier if we'd found one wearing reindeer ears but the Santa hat worked, didn't it?

I wish you could see me, Evie, as I write this. I'm sitting here grinning ear-to-ear because I'm reliving all these memories, too. I guess I'm getting a double dose of happiness because I can also close my eyes and picture the future. I can picture you standing in front of a big beautiful tree. I can see you smile as you hang the final ornament. I can picture you reading this letter, maybe for the second time LOL!, and I'm grateful that, even if it is just in a small way, we can still share this holiday together...one more time.

We had so many good times together, didn't we?

Don't let the good times stop.

Please, Evie.

That brings me to request number three: I want you to promise to purchase a brand new ornament this year. Something with special meaning for you. Something that will bring a smile to your face in years to come and create one of your first new Christmas memories.

I know you well enough to know moving on isn't easy for you. I also know you're strong enough to do it.

So enjoy this Christmas, sweetheart. Enjoy today.

Go on, get busy. You've got a tree to pick out, a house to decorate, a special ornament to buy.

Oh yeah, and don't forget to dress Pug up in his reindeer ears. It wouldn't be Christmas without it.

One more thing...

I love you, Evie.

Merry Christmas, Bryan.

Eve sat on the edge of the bed and took a couple deep breaths. Her eyes burned with unshed tears at the same time as a bittersweet smile tugged at her mouth. The letter was beautiful, simply beautiful. Bryan knew her so well and knew exactly what she'd need to hear to help get her through this first holiday without him. She lowered the letter to her lap and looked over at Pug.

"Well, there you have it, Pug. The love of our life is saying good-bye, isn't he? He's telling us it's all right to be happy. It's all right to move on." No longer able to hold back the tears, she swiped them away as they rolled down her face. "As sick as he was, he still thought about us. So now we have to be strong and think about him, don't we?"

Eve pointed her index finger at the dog. "And you heard him loud and clear. He wants you to wear those reindeer ears, buddy, so don't even try and fight me on it. The first good opportunity I get, you're going to be Rudolph the Pug."

Pug didn't seem to know what she was saying but he also didn't seem to want to chance sitting around to find out. She watched him get up and slink out of the bedroom like a thief in the night.

Eve laughed out loud. It felt good to laugh. She kissed the folded letter and then slid it into her night table drawer where she'd stored the first letter. She wanted to read it again, and again, before she'd be able to pack it away. Bryan knew her so well.

Thank you, Bryan. A warmth and sense of peace engulfed her. *Yep, he was still here.*

Eve stood up and yelled, "Pug, get back here. We're going out. We have some shopping to do and a tree to buy."

Seven

"Daddy! Hurry, come look!" Katie rushed into the barn and pulled up short at the table where Michael sat going over work orders. The child grabbed his coat sleeve and pulled. "Hurry, Daddy. Come on."

Michael steadied the papers he'd been working on, put a paper weight on top so they couldn't blow away, and stood. "Okay, Katie. Calm down. What's got you all excited?"

"Ms. Eve is here in her really, really big truck and Pug's here, too."

Eve was here? She hadn't answered any of his phone messages. He'd begun to think their budding friendship was too much too soon for her. But she was here? A wave of delight swept over him.

His daughter tugged on his jacket. "C'mon, Daddy, before she thinks nobody is here and she goes away."

He allowed Katie to drag him across the barn floor though, truthfully, he didn't need to be dragged. He had all he could do not to race his daughter to the truck, and then realized just how ridiculous that thought was. What was it about this woman that made him feel like an adolescent boy? No. Fast forward to college age. His thoughts about this woman weren't anywhere as innocent as a teen hoping to take a girl to the prom.

When they cleared the barn, he grinned. Danny, his mom, and his dad already had Eve surrounded. So much for his daughter's worries that Eve would think no one was home.

Eve looked his way and watched him cross the yard. Her smile lit up her whole face and a funny, jumpy feeling started in the pit of his stomach. Glints of sunlight hit her auburn hair. The chilly winter day kissed her cheeks with a rosy glow. As he drew near, her eyes sparkled and he knew she was happy to see him, too.

"Hello, Michael. I've decided to put up a Christmas tree this year. Your family has been kind enough to educate me on the different types of evergreen trees and how to pick the one best suited for me."

"Good to see you, Eve. I'm glad we can be of help."

"Miss Eve, can Pug come out of the truck and play with me? Please," Katie asked.

Pug pressed his already flattened face against the car window. He appeared as excited to get out of the cab and see the girl as the child was to see him.

Eve laughed. She opened the cab door, unlatched Pug's seat belt, and lowered the dog to the ground. She handed Katie the leash. "Be careful, Katie. I don't want Pug to get too excited and start to pull you. You could fall."

Katie, already running with the leash and Pug in hand toward the tree farm, yelled back over her shoulder, "It's okay, Miss Eve. We're just going to play. I won't fall."

Eve shot a wary look Michael's way.

He grinned. "Not to worry. Your dog seems to have a genuine soft spot for Katie. He proved that on Main Street. I think he'll behave himself. There's plenty of property for them to run and play without getting into any mischief."

"But if he pulls her too hard and she falls…"

"She's a kid. Kids fall. Matter of fact, Katie made a point of telling me after our skating outing last Sunday that it didn't hurt when she falls. So…" He laughed and shrugged his shoulders.

"He's right, my dear." Ruth patted her shoulder. "If I had a nickel for every scrape or cut my kids got growing up, I could have retired years ago."

Everyone laughed but Katie still strained to keep the child and dog in sight.

"You're here to pick out a tree, right?" Michael asked.

Eve nodded.

"Well, let's follow them," he suggested. "They're headed straight into the tree farm. Maybe you'll find the tree of your dreams while keeping them in plain sight as well."

"Sounds like a plan," Eve said. "I have to move my truck, though. I'm blocking the main drive."

"Throw me your keys." Danny stretched out a palm. "I'll pull it over and park it for you. I've been dying to get behind the wheel of one of these monster trucks, anyway."

She gave him the keys and he hopped into the cab.

"Let's go," Sean McGruder said. "I've got several trees to show you that I think you'll like."

Ruth clasped her husband's arm and kept him in place. "Why don't we let Michael show Eve the trees, dear?"

"What? Why? I'm the one who leads the tours."

Ruth smiled at Eve and then looked back at her husband. "I know dear, but I have a special project I need your help with in the kitchen." She started to pull him away. "Michael is perfectly capable of helping her find a tree."

"The kitchen? For heaven's sake, woman, why on earth do you need me in your kitchen?"

"You'll see, dear." She led her husband toward the house but called over her shoulder. "I've got a pot roast cooking, Eve. We'd love you to join us for dinner when you've finished your tree shopping if you'd like."

"That's very kind but certainly not necessary Mrs. McGruder."

The older couple had reached the porch steps and paused, Sean McGruder's unintelligible protests floating on the air between them. "Nonsense," Ruth said. "What's one more plate? We'll see you after your outing." The couple climbed the steps, then paused again. "Take your time. And call me Ruth." She waved and the two of them disappeared inside.

Michael grinned. "My mother means well but subtlety is not one of her assets."

Eve returned his smile and the two of them walked in the direction Katie and Pug had gone.

"I owe you an apology," Eve said.

He raised an eyebrow but remained silent as they continued walking.

"I never returned your calls."

"No apologies needed. I understand. I was just reaching out as a friend to see if you were doing okay." He smiled. "Now that you're here in person, how are you doing?"

Eve ducked her head and seemed to be pondering how to answer the question. "I'm fine. I admit I've had a few moments, here and there, where it's been a bit tough but..." She looked up and there it was again—that radiant smile of hers. "Someone very close to me has been helping me through things."

"Good. Glad to hear it. Nobody should be navigating through the holidays on their own the first year after a loss. It's not easy."

Eve nodded agreement. "No, it isn't."

Michael spotted his daughter and the dog not far ahead. They continued to follow at a slow but steady pace behind. Michael pointed out the varied types of trees they saw as they passed through different areas of the farm. He asked her a few questions. What was she looking for in a tree? Had she seen anything she'd liked so far? If she could give him a more detailed idea about what she wanted, he'd have a better idea how to steer her to a tree she might like.

"Don't know," she said.

Michael grinned. "You do realize that we have about 1500 trees per acre and we farm 20 acres."

Eve's brow puckered. "May I ask you a personal question?" She continued when he nodded. "Between the lot on Main Street and the people who come out here to pick their own trees is it enough to sustain you for the rest of the year or do all of you have to have other jobs, too?"

Michael chuckled. "Nope. Trees are pretty much it."

"But how...?"

"We run both a catalog and an online e-business. Mom takes care of most of that end of it. Danny takes on the responsibility of filling the orders and getting them shipped. I do the billing."

"Wow! I didn't know you could sell Christmas trees that way."

"Not all our trees are grown for Christmas. During the year we sell lumber to be made into furniture and, sometimes, we sell lumber to paper mills."

"Wow, that's interesting. I had no idea you could sell trees all year round."

"I'm glad we can. I like to eat." Michael laughed. "Between what we sell here, in town, online and via catalog, we do just fine during the holidays, too. Now why don't we catch up with our little ones and get you a tree?"

Michael pointed out a variety of fir trees and pine trees. Eve looked at Douglas Firs and Scotch Pines. He discussed the density and strength of limbs as well as which trees lost their needles and which trees carried the most scent.

Eve was fascinated. She wandered down rows and rows of trees finding it harder than ever before to pick out just one.

"We could be out here until Christmas next year has come and gone if you insist on seeing each and every tree," he teased.

She waved her hand at him. "Don't rush me. I'll know it when I see it."

"I wouldn't think of rushing you. I haven't walked the entire twenty acres in several years. I need the exercise." He fought to keep his lips from twisting into a grin.

She shot him a look, stuck out her tongue, then continued shopping as if his questions and concerns held no merit.

So what's the lesson here? Don't get between a woman and her shopping spree? Ok, got it. Don't try to suggest any particular tree to her because she'll know it when she sees it? Check. He squelched the chuckle rising in his throat.

They meandered up one row of trees and down another. Katie and Pug romping and racing together but within view. He'd bet both child and dog would sleep well tonight. That is, if they didn't collapse from exhaustion while Ms.-Can't-Decide keeps shopping. As they walked, his curiosity got the better of him. "Mind if I ask a question?"

Eve laughed. "Isn't that what you've been doing for the last ten minutes? Do I have a particular type of tree in mind? Do I like the color of a spruce tree? Would I prefer a Douglas Fir or a Scotch Pine or maybe a Balsam Fir? Do I want branches that slope down sharply or fatter trees with branches that reach out like arms? Do I want a dense tree so it needs fewer ornaments or do I want a tree with plenty of space between branches for tons of ornaments?" She giggled. "I could swear I've been volleying questions galore so why not one more?"

Her eyes shone brightly. Her genuine smile warmed his heart. She was enjoying herself and his stupidity had almost blown it with a question he really had no right to ask.

"What?" She stopped walking and studied him. "Hey, I was only kidding. I don't mind your questions. How else am I going to find the perfect tree?" She tilted her head and her expression sobered at his continued hesitation. "This isn't about the trees, is it?"

"Forget I mentioned anything. Let's catch up with Katie and your fur baby."

"My fur baby? Pug? You've got to be kidding. He's Bryan's dog and he never misses an opportunity to remind me of that fact."

Michael reached out to cup her elbow and lead her on the path but she gently pulled back.

"You're not getting off that easily, buddy. Ask me. What do you want to know?" She stared him down.

"This isn't the time or place..."

"Michael, you've started it. Now you have to finish it." She smiled up into his eyes. "What are you afraid of? I don't bite. What do you want to ask me?"

"I'm sorry, Eve. I was going to ask you about your husband. I was wondering what kind of guy he was. How long you were married. How he died." He lowered his eyes. He felt so guilty for ruining her day. "I don't know what I was thinking. I'm supposed to be helping distract you from bad memories not bring them up. Some friend I'm turning out to be."

She looked at him intensely. "Bryan will never be a bad memory for me, Michael, just his death will, and it's normal for you to wonder about him."

Michael's gut took a hit. "Oh, God, Eve, I wasn't suggesting Bryan was a bad memory. I just meant..." He shuffled his feet and stared at the ground. "Sorry. Please. Forget I said anything. Sometimes I'm great at putting my foot in my mouth."

Eve gently placed her hand on his forearm. "It's okay. Really." She smiled at him. "I enjoy talking about Bryan. He was a really funny, warm, loving man. I will always cherish the memories I have of our life together."

Michael nodded approvingly. "As it should be."

"We were married for fourteen years. But we met in kindergarten." They slowly resumed walking up the trail. "Bryan fell on my art project and ruined the Christmas card I was making for my parents. I was so angry I hit him and started to cry."

"Wow. Poor guy. He really got off to a bad start with you, didn't he?" Michael laughed.

"Oh, he made amends. He gave me a bag of M&M candy out of his lunch box. The teacher helped me glue the candy on the paper. I ended up with the best decorated tree in the room."

Michael grinned. "Now that's what I call a save." He shot a glance her way. "So you grew up together?"

"Yep. Best friends. I was a bit of a tomboy which helped. I found it fun to play ball, ride bikes, play in mud, and swing on tire ropes. When we got older…well, like I said, we were BFF's. We told each other everything. We had each other's back through thick and thin. If anyone hurt or messed with one of us, the other would appear, almost out of nowhere, and we'd present a united front." Eve laughed. "We were two peas in a pod and it was an awesome time in my life."

Michael listened intently. He married his wife when he was 35. He'd already sown all his wild oats and he was ready to settle down. They'd been married for six years before he lost her and that was almost five years ago. Her death had knocked him to his knees. There were times he hadn't thought he would ever be able to stand up, again. He couldn't imagine how much more difficult it would be to have actually grown up with the love of your life, to have shared a lifetime of memories before your adult lifetime even began.

"I'm sorry," he said, feeling the words inadequate but having nothing else to offer.

"I'm not." She smiled, a genuine smile which lit her face and eyes. "Bryan and I were blessed. We had it all. We had a wonderful life shoved into the first half of a normal person's lifetime. I wouldn't trade one second of our time together. How can I ever be sorry about that?"

"I get it."

They walked a little further in silence. Almost as if she could read his mind, she answered the questions he still hadn't asked.

"The first eleven years of our marriage were a slice of heaven on earth. Don't get me wrong. We had arguments and disagreements like all couples about many things…trivial things…things so trivial I don't even remember what they were about." She grinned. "I can remember the shouting and yelling, the slammed doors, the anger." Genuine mirth lit her eyes. "But I remember making up more." She glanced his way and a beautiful flush spread from her neck up her face giving credence to that memory.

"I hear you," Michael said. "My wife and I had a rule. We would never go to bed angry." He grinned. "I spent many a night on the sofa before I was allowed back in bed again."

They both laughed.

"You said the first eleven years were heaven but you were married fourteen…" he prompted.

Eve's eyes clouded but the smile stayed on her face. "I wouldn't change one day of the first eleven years of our marriage. But when Bryan was diagnosed with lung cancer, everything changed. Life took a spin we hadn't anticipated. These kinds of problems weren't supposed to surface until we were old and gray. But I guess the Lord had other plans."

"Bryan faced his cancer diagnosis the same way he lived his life—with optimism, determination, and a strength I'm not sure I would have had. He carried the fear for both of us." She pondered silently for a few minutes before retelling the story. "At first, we did everything the doctors told us. Chemo. Radiation. Removal of a part of Bryan's left lung. He lost about twenty pounds as well as all of his beautiful, thick brown hair. But that didn't get him down. He bragged about his flat though flabby abs, and actually drew funny sayings and designs in henna on his bald head."

She laughed out loud at the memory and the light in her eyes danced. "And he beat it. He went into remission. His hair grew back. His weight came back. His smile grew into a full-fledged grin wherever he went. Life was good, again. But it wasn't the same. We'd grown up. We developed a deeper understanding of how fragile and fleeting life can be…at any age. We decided not to ever take another day for granted."

Eve took a few steps forward, prompting him to join her, then continued talking.

"Bryan and I bought a small camper and spent that summer traveling. He was a software designer. His company presented him with the opportunity to work from home. I was able to continue my editing business. We didn't have any financial concerns. Life was good, better than good. It was a wonderful summer, our last wonderful summer."

Her eyes glistened. "That winter the cancer came back with a vengeance. It had metastasized, spreading to his right lung, his bones, and finally his brain. The last two years of Bryan's life consisted of hospitals, surgeries, treatments that ripped his insides out, horrific pain, so bad that near the very end not even morphine could touch it." She swiped a tear away.

"Bryan accepted the reality of his situation before me. He insisted he be brought home. He wanted his last months to be surrounded by me, his family, and Pug—not in a hospital, hooked up to machines. So we did. We called in hospice to help with his personal care and keep him comfortable. They were a God send. They took care of Bryan and they offered fabulous emotional support for me.

Bryan's parents and siblings came every day. We set up a schedule so everyone got to spend individual time with him without overwhelming or tiring him too much. He was rarely alone." She was quiet for several minutes but soon she continued.

"We moved his hospital bed in front of the sliding glass doors facing the back yard so we could open them on nice days and we could sit in the sun together. We listened to music. I read him books. He held Pug. He held me." Her voice broke. "I was curled up on the bed in his arms the night he kissed me, closed his eyes and left."

Michael didn't say a word. He simply put his arms around her and pulled her close, offering comfort the only way he could.

"Bryan had been in such horrible pain at the end. Every bone in his body in agony. When he passed, I felt such a wave of relief." She swiped away her tears. "For him, of course, not me. All I could think about was that all of his pain and suffering was finally over."

"I'm so sorry, Eve," Michael said.

She smiled through her tears. "Our love for each other, Michael, was such a gift." She leaned into his hug, seemed almost grateful for the comfort. He hoped he made her feel safe, protected. She eased out of his arms and drew a tissue from her coat pocket. "Bryan's family, and mine, of course, helped me through the worst of it." She threw a glance over her shoulder. "You have a wonderful family. I'm sure they were a great help to you when you lost your wife."

"Understatement of the year. Don't know how I would have gotten through that first year without them, or the years since, truthfully. They've been wonderful."

A new understanding grew between them and they walked in companionable silence as Eve perused one tree and studied another. After a bit, she asked, "Do you mind if I ask how you lost your wife?"

"A head-on collision coming back from her six-week check-up after Katie was born. Katie had been in the back in her car seat. It was a miracle she hadn't been killed, too."

Eve gasped. "Oh, Michael, that's horrible. I'm so sorry."

Even after all these years, those memories could still tug at his heart. "Thank you. It was the hardest thing that has ever happened to me. I wasn't sure what hurt the most—the finality of her death or the fact that I never got the chance to say good-bye or remind her how much I loved her. But..." He stopped and waited for Eve to face him. "Life continues, Eve, whether you want it to or not, and you learn to move on with it. Not easily. Not quickly, either. You take one step forward, sometimes two steps back. But inevitably, the pain and grief fade away. Survival depends on it, doesn't it?" He smiled at her. "But the memories last. No one can take them away from you. You'll learn to cherish them. I promise."

Eve nodded. "I already do."

He wished he could wave a magic wand, sprinkle her with holiday magic, and make all of the pain disappear. But he knew through first-hand experience it wasn't possible.

"Remember, the offer still stands, I'm here if you ever want to talk. If you'd prefer a female perspective, my mom is a great listener. I know for a fact, she'd be first in line to step up to the plate to try and help." He leaned forward and stage whispered. "I think that's part of the reason for tonight's pot roast invitation."

Eve chuckled. "I sort of got that feeling."

The sound of a child's laughter and a dog barking filled the air. They looked up. Katie ran out between two trees, no leash in hand, but Pug close on her heels. Then Pug raced back the other way with Katie chasing behind.

"I can't believe it." Eve's expression showed surprise. "I don't think I've ever heard Pug bark. Not happily, anyway. He'll growl or bark when complaining, which is frequently I might add, but he truly seems to be enjoying himself."

"Pug must have fallen under Katie's spell. She loves dogs." He grinned. "Santa whispered in my ear that this is the year he's bringing her a puppy of her own."

Eve clapped her hands together. "I'm really happy to hear it. She's going to be one very happy child on Christmas morning. What kind of dog are you getting?"

"That's still being debated."

She shot him a quizzical glance.

"My parents want her to get a puppy. Her fifth birthday is the first week in January. I think a puppy will be too much work and responsibility for a child so young. I'm leaning heavily on adopting a rescue dog."

"That's a great idea, Michael. There are so many wonderful dogs out there that need a home. Finding a dog already house broken and maybe just a little older and less rambunctious than a puppy might be a better fit for Katie."

"My thoughts exactly." He looked at her. "Hey, you're a dog owner. Maybe you could come with me and help me make a good selection. What do you think?"

"Me?" She placed her palm on her chest and chuckled. "I'm taking care of a dog who hates my guts and won't give me the time of day. I'm not sure I'd be the best one to help you choose a dog for your daughter."

Michael shrugged. "Well, maybe I'll take you with me anyway. I'll encourage the dogs to give you a sniff test. If any of them seems to hate you, then that's the one I'll pick. After all, it certainly is working with Pug."

Eve looked surprised, then she threw her head back and belly laughed. "Okay," she said, waving her hand in the air once she was able to get her laughter under control. "I get it. I'd love to go with you."

"Great. I'll call and we'll set up a time." He hesitated. "But, you know, there's just one catch."

She raised an eyebrow.

"You'll have to answer the call."

She grinned and nodded her agreement. "Point taken." She reached out and gently touched his forearm. "I'd love to help you choose a pet for Katie. Thank you for asking me."

"I'd love to help you pick out a Christmas tree," he said. "Hopefully, sometime this year," he muttered under his breath.

Eve chuckled and shot him an evil eye.

He pretended innocence. "What? I'm volunteering to help. What do you say?"

"I say what's taking you so long? Let's go."

They began looking in earnest for the best tree on the farm.

Eight

"Are you sure we can't change your mind, dear?" Ruth smiled warmly. "It would only take a second to pull out another plate. The pot roast and biscuits are done. My husband's uncorking the wine. We'd love to have you join us."

"I appreciate it, Ruth. A home-cooked meal on a cold winter night sounds heavenly."

"Good. Then you'll stay?"

"I can't. Not tonight. I promised someone very dear to me that I would do something for them, today." Eve smiled at the older woman. "But that mouth-watering aroma is making it very difficult to say no. Can I take a rain check for the next time you cook pot roast?"

Ruth nodded. "Of course. You're welcome any time."

After everyone exchanged good-byes, Michael walked Eve and Pug out to her truck. Michael tethered Pug into the passenger seat before he walked around to the driver's side of the cab. He chuckled but was smart enough not to offer assistance as he watched Eve try to swing her tiny frame into the monster truck cab. It took more than one try but, eventually, she was successful.

Once settled behind the steering wheel, she lowered the window and grinned. "I bet you didn't think I'd make it up here without help, did you?"

Michael raised his hands. "I never doubted you for a minute."

"Liar." Her grin widened. "At least, you were wise enough to keep your doubts to yourself." Her expression sobered. "Seriously, Michael, thank you."

"For?" He shot her a quizzical look.

"Everything. I know this is your busiest time of year and I took up a lot of it today. You showed exceptional patience while helping me find the perfect tree. Even offering to bring the tree out to my house tomorrow and set it up for me."

He grinned. "All in a day's work."

"And the sensitive and deep conversations, the encouragement, that's all in a day's work, too?"

"No." He smiled up into her eyes. "That's called being a good friend."

"Well, good friend, thank you. Again. For everything."

He waved two fingers in a mock salute. "Take care, Eve. Drive safely. I'll bring the tree by your place around noon tomorrow if that time works for you."

She nodded her agreement.

"Don't forget you promised to go dog shopping with me after we set up your tree."

Eve chuckled. "I haven't forgotten. But Christmas is still two weeks away. What are you going to do if you find the perfect dog? It's supposed to be a Christmas present."

"I'll cross that bridge when I come to it. This gift is too important to leave it go to the last minute. I might not find the right pet for Katie on the first try and I may need the extra time to keep looking."

Eve realized she understood this man more than she thought she could in such a short period of time. He's a hard worker and puts in long hours without complaint. He's devoted to both his daughter and his family. He is comfortable in his own skin. He knows she thinks he's hot, because he is, but he isn't conceited enough to play on her mixed emotions about it. He likes to plan things well in advance but demonstrates flexibility, exhibited in shopping for the new pet for his daughter. He has all the makings of being a great friend for those lucky enough to be included in his inner circle. He responds well to unexpected circumstances.

Who else could catch a flying pug in his lap, not be angry, and actually share his sandwich with the dog?

And did she say he's hot? God forgive her but all her female parts screamed the entire afternoon to acknowledge just how hot. A warm flush crept up her neck. She chanced a glance his way. It was almost as if he could read her mind. The knowing glint in his eyes and the smile on his face only deepened her embarrassment.

Eve settled into the driver's seat and offered a weak wave out the window. She hurriedly turned the key in the ignition. "Gotta run."

"Don't run too far, Eve," his deep, rumbling voice reached her ears like a warm caress. "I'm going to be on your doorstep tomorrow at noon."

Promises. Promises.

Her blush deepened. She nodded, rolled up her window, and drove the truck down the driveway. No matter how hard she tried, she couldn't erase her anticipation of this six foot hunk of a man arriving on her doorstep tomorrow.

Christmas presents come in all shapes and sizes, don't they?
She'd like hers best served hot.
Oh yeah! Hot, hot, hot.

As Eve neared Main Street, she glanced over at Pug, who was sound asleep on the front seat. She grinned. Poor dog had to be exhausted not to be plastering his already flattened face against the glass as they drove. She couldn't remember a time, at least not one in the past year, when the dog had played so actively or seemed so happy.

Katie was a gift.

Eve knew Pug grieved for Bryan, the poor dog had his own struggles finding a new normal. But Pug seemed to perk up and forget his grief, for just a little while, whenever he was with Katie. She knew it didn't mean he was forgetting Bryan. It just meant that Pug was allowing a little bit of happy back into his life.

Who am I kidding? It's not just Pug who is feeling little snatches of happy. It's me and I'm feeling guilty as hell. I'm attracted to a handsome man. I'm attracted not only to his looks but also his kind and generous personality. And I shouldn't be. I can't be. Can I?

If she didn't know better, she could almost hear Bryan laughing. She could hear him goading her to go back and re-read his letters. What part was she missing? The part where he told her he didn't want her to feel guilty about anything? Or the part where he told her how much he wanted her to be happy? Or maybe it was the part where he told her he hoped she had made some new friends?

Michael definitely qualified as a new friend. That wasn't the problem. It was hoping that new friend becomes something more.

She eased the truck into the first available spot she'd seen big enough to house this monstrosity. One of these days she'd have to sell it. It was crazy to keep a truck just to drive a dog around town. But she didn't have to make that decision today.

Baby steps.

She woke Pug, fastened on his leash, and the two of them ambled up Main Street. It was dusk and she had to admit her timing was perfect. Although people dotted the street and wandered in and out of the shops, the majority of the people were home eating their dinner and would come out later tonight.

The thought of dinner triggered a growl in her belly. When was the last time she ate? She'd grabbed a coffee to go at breakfast and had missed lunch as she spent her afternoon shopping for her new Christmas tree. Pug was probably starved, too. She hadn't fed herself and she definitely hadn't fed him. She hoped he would behave himself on this brief stop and was too sleepy to attack the first person he saw with food.

Eve briefly considered calling off this particular shopping trip. She could always come back tomorrow…or even the next day. She still had two and a half weeks until Christmas.

But Bryan's letter, his words, his wishes weighed heavily on her heart.

She tied Pug's leash to the post in front of the Old Christmas Shoppe. "I'll only be a minute, Pug. I have to pick up an ornament. It won't take long. So please, please, please be good. If you don't try to steal anyone's food, I promise to fix you a meal fit for a king. Okay, boy? Tonight will be people food for Pug. But only if you sit here and behave yourself. Got it?"

The dog just stared up at her.

Okay, Eve, get a grip. You keep talking to this dog like he understands every word. You better start spending more time with humans who really can understand what you say.

Eve threw one more worried glance in Pug's direction then turned and hurried into the store. She started glancing at one ornament after another. She picked up a lovely sparkling gold glass ball. She'd get this. Then her eye caught a bird house covered with snow and holly. This one's cute.

What had Michael called me earlier, Ms.-Can't-Decide?

Annoyed with herself for not being able to choose, she decided to buy them both. She needed to get out of here before Pug gets into trouble. But as she moved toward the cash register, a twinkling light in her peripheral vision caught her eye, bringing her to a full stop. She stared at it for a full minute.

Really?

A smile tugged at her lips. She walked over to the display and gingerly lifted the ornament in her fingers. The tiny lit up gazebo rested on a snow drift overlooking a small pond covered with extremely miniature ice skaters. It reminded her of her day skating with Michael.

She remembered the warmth of his breath on her neck, the masculine weight of his hand on her waist, the safe haven of his body as he held her close and glided across the ice.

She stared at the gazebo in quiet awe. Bryan's letter had asked her to pick out something new. Something special. Something that would bring a happy memory in the years to come of this particular Christmas. She unhooked the ornament from the display.

Her heart thumped an extra beat and her smile grew. If it hadn't been for that glint of light, she would have left the store and missed seeing what she knew was the perfect choice.

Coincidence? Maybe but she didn't think so.

After paying, she watched the cashier place all three ornaments in a bag and hand them to her. Excited and happy about her purchases, she rushed out the door to collect Pug. But not before she gave credit where credit was due.

Thank you, Bryan.

Nine

Eve stumbled over her own feet as she made her way across the foyer while trying to pull her cell phone out of her coat pocket. She caught the call on its final ring.

"Hey, Mom. How's everyone in sunny Florida?" Eve tucked her cell phone between her shoulder and cheek. She eased out of coat and tossed it on the sofa. Lifting the small table in front of the picture window in the den, she carried it over and placed it adjacent to the fireplace. "What do you mean I sound happy? Of course, I'm happy. Don't you want me to sound happy?"

Eve chuckled as her mother stumbled over her words trying to apologize.

"Relax, Mom. It's fine. I'm fine. Yes, really."

Eve picked up a small chair and placed it beside the table. She eyed the combo and, deciding one more chair was needed, carried a second one over to the grouping.

"Why am I happy?" Eve stopped what she was doing and laughed. "It's Christmas, Mom. Holiday cheer and Christmas spirit, right?" Satisfied with the grouping, she plopped into one of the chairs and transferred the phone to her hand. "Besides, I had breakfast with my friend, Julie, this morning. She's leaving for the holidays to see her parents and it was our last chance to catch up before she leaves. We had a good time. So, tell me, what's new with you guys?"

For the next few minutes, she listened to a day-by-day itinerary of their activities. Her mom truly was enjoying being with her grandchildren this holiday and Eve offered a silent prayer of gratitude to both God and Connie for making this happen. This holiday was a series of highs and lows for Eve. Her mom didn't need to be subjected to her mood swings. Heck, she wished she didn't have to put up with such highs and lows herself.

"What am I doing?" Eve smiled. "I'm waiting for my Christmas tree to be delivered."

Her mother's happy squeal and succession of questions made Eve smile even more.

"I know I said I wasn't going to put up a tree but I changed my mind." She listened to the barrage of questions. What made her change her mind? Where did she buy the tree? Who was going to put it up for her?

"Mom, it's no big deal. Bryan and I always put up a tree. Even when he was at his sickest, he wanted to be able to lie in bed and look at the tree all lit up and decorated." She tried to hide the hint of sadness creeping into her voice at the memory. "Bryan would want me to put up a tree this year, too. So that's what I'm going to do." She listened to her mom agree and barrage her with another round of questions.

"Where'd I buy the tree? McGruder's Tree Farm. Yes, it's the same place Bryan and I got our tree every year. Good memory, Mom. That is the last name of the man Pug jumped on and stole his sandwich. What do you mean it's a sign?" Eve rolled her eyes and looked at the ceiling. "I'd like to think Bryan is too busy being happy in Heaven to worry about sending me signs. Me? I'd say it's a coincidence. Small world, maybe?"

"Okay, okay." Eve got to her feet and headed toward the picture window. "You call it a sign. I'll call it a coincidence and we'll both be happy. Gotta run now, Mom. The man will be here any minute with the tree and I don't have the room ready yet. Give Connie and the family my love. Talk to you soon. Bye."

She punched the button on her cell phone and breathed a sigh of relief. She slid her fingertips into the back pockets of her jeans and assessed the empty spot in front of the den picture window. In years past, Brian had set up their tree in the living room so it would be visible to anyone coming in the front door.

This year...

This year had to be different, new.

She opened her arms and walked in a circle in the empty space trying to imitate the width of the tree.

"What do you think, Pug? Think the tree will fit if we put it in here?" She threw a glance over her shoulder and chastised herself.

I'm talking to the dog, again. I don't know what's worse—the belief that Pug understands everything I say or the unspoken belief that someday he might actually answer me.

Right on cue, Pug woofed.

Eve startled. Her eyes widened and her breath caught in her throat but before she could read more into Pug's woof, she heard a heavy truck door slam. She slid open the drapes, leaned to the left and looked out at the driveway. She recognized the truck instantly, and then glanced at her watch. If anything, the man was punctual. Noon on the dot.

The doorbell rang. Pug made a mad dash from the room and was already woofing and scratching at the front door when she got there. Eve ran her fingers through her hair, took a glance in the hall mirror at her hair, and then straightened her Frosty the Snowman sweater over her hips.

What am I doing? Eve gulped in a deep breath. *I'm answering the front door and welcoming in a new friend. That's what I'm doing.*

She hoped Michael wouldn't pick up on her nervousness. She opened the door, and the moment she saw him standing there, the fake smile she'd planted on her face slid into a real one. Every cell in her body reacted to the sight of this tall, handsome hunk. He leaned a shoulder on her doorframe, crossed his arms and grinned. "You look festive."

She glanced down at her sweater, then returned the grin. "Just wait until you see me decked out in my Mrs. Claus surrounded by all her Christmas pies sweater."

His eyes took their time traveling over her body and his gaze almost felt like a warm, physical caress. The glint in those beautiful sapphire eyes telegraphed his appreciation of the view. She refused to dwell on why that thought made her happy. A thick batch of black hair stuck out from beneath his winter cap and fell in a wave across his forehead. It was all she could do not to reach out and curl a lock of it around her index finger.

He looked at her intently. If she didn't know better, she'd believe he could see right through her, read her every thought and mood. But it was that mischievous grin slashing across his mouth and drawing her attention to his lips that caused a warmth to spread through her body—despite her censoring mind trying it's hardest to ruin the moment.

"Hello, Michael." She heard the huskiness in her voice and she blushed.

Before any awkwardness could form between them, Michael glanced down at his feet. "And hi to you, buddy." He bent down and rubbed Pug's belly who was flopping around on the ground like a fish out of water. "You look pretty spiffy, too, in your Santa sweater." He looked up at Eve. "I'm starting to feel underdressed."

"We can fix that. If there's one thing I have, it's plenty of holiday sweaters." She choked on the words almost the second they passed her lips. What was she thinking? She couldn't lend out one of Bryan's sweaters to anyone.

He raised his palms in surrender. "Whoa, thanks but no thanks. I'll pass." He shooed Pug back into the house, stood up and grinned. "By the way, my father said to tell you that you picked out the best tree on our farm."

Eve chuckled. "I bet he says that to every one of his customers."

He shrugged. "What can I say? Dad believes if the customer is satisfied with the tree they picked, then to them it is the best one, right?"

"Point taken."

He clapped his hands together. "So are you ready for me to bring your prize winner in?"

"Sure. Let me grab my coat and gloves and I'll help you." She started to turn away when she felt him grasp her elbow. A fresh rush of heat rushed through her body at his touch.

Get over it, already. She scolded herself.

She'd never been attracted to any man in her entire life other than Bryan. These feelings were new. Scary. Awesome.

"I've got this," Michael said.

She turned back to face him and that crooked grin of his stole her breath away.

"I do this all the time," he said.

What? Send waves of heat coursing through a woman's body? Steal a woman's breath? Make a woman fantasize about what those large masculine hands would feel like roaming over her body?

"The tree is tied up," Michael said. "It won't be a problem. I've got a large dolly and I can wheel it right in."

Tied up? Wheeling what right in?

Eve's cheeks flamed and her breathing shallowed.

Michael cocked his head and looked at her. "Are you all right?"

She nodded.

"Okay." He still didn't look like he fully accepted her answer but moved on nonetheless. "You can help by holding the door open for me and then pointing where you want me to set up the tree."

He left and was back again within minutes.

Eve opened the door wide and her eyes wider. She hadn't remembered picking out a tree this big. It was huge! He amazed her with how well he was in control, even though the tree, looming at least a foot and a half over his head, was tied and on a dolly. A welcome scent of pine quickly followed by a blast of cold air filled the foyer. She shut the door behind him, hurried ahead, and led Michael into the den.

With a little struggle here and there, the two of them secured the tree into the stand she had waiting and they positioned it in front of the window.

When they finished, Michael shrugged out of his coat and tossed it over the back of a chair. "Dad was right. You definitely got the best tree we had." Fisted hands on hips, he perused it up and down. "But I'm sorry to say it still needs a little something."

"It does?" She played along with him. "Water in the base of the tree stand, maybe?"

He quickly rummaged through the open boxes resting on the recliner, end table, and floor. He turned and held up his prize. "Here we go. Lights." He grinned. "May I?"

She hesitated for a heartbeat. Putting the lights on the tree had always been Bryan's job. But Bryan wasn't here to do it this year, was he? A pang hit her heart but she smiled anyway.

"Sure," she said. "Knock yourself out." She silently watched him start to unravel the cords and set to work weaving the lights through the branches. Memories collided with new feelings she still refused to name and she didn't know whether to laugh or cry. Her emotions threatened to run away with her, and the last thing she wanted to do was say or do something awkward or embarrassing. She knew she needed a moment to herself to gather her thoughts so she could try and deal with her confusion, her ever-present nagging guilt, and grief…grief she'd believed she had under control. Until she didn't.

Panic growing by the second, she turned and made a beeline for the kitchen. "Can I offer you a cup of coffee or tea?" she called over her shoulder.

So engrossed in his project, Michael seemed totally oblivious to her impending panic. Without looking away from the job at hand, he asked, "What are you having?"

"Cinnamon Apple Tea. It…it relaxes me on cold winter days."

Michael continued wrapping the first strand of lights through the branches. "Relaxation works for me. I'll take what you're having. Thanks."

Eve couldn't race out of the room fast enough.

He'd have what she's having?

She's having a personal war of emotions and, truthfully, not having any idea which side she wanted to win the battle. Her heart hurt, literally hurt, seeing the tree up and another man decorating it. She missed Bryan. It should be Bryan trimming that tree. It wasn't fair.

But it also wasn't fair that a toned, fit, fabulous man stood in her den merely yards away and all she could think about was running her finger tips along his unshaven face, feeling his biceps throb beneath her hands as she traced a path up and down his arms, and those lips…

Yeah, it was pretty elementary what she had to do.

Panic time 101.

Ten

Eve leaned heavily against the kitchen sink, closed her eyes, and drew in one very long, deep breath. Her head pounded. Her pulse raced. Her eyes burned with unshed tears.

What am I doing?

She missed Bryan so much. An ache and emptiness dwelled deep in her heart and soul. In some ways she knew those places would always be filled with love and loss and memories of Bryan.

But she also felt an attraction—an unexpected, exciting, new attraction—for this handsome, kind, sweet man currently putting the lights on her Christmas tree.

How am I supposed to handle this? What am I supposed to be feeling? Is it too soon to be feeling any attraction for any man? And what is Michael thinking about me? Did I misread things? Didn't I see genuine attraction, maybe even desire, gazing back at me…waiting…letting me steer the course and the speed?

She rubbed her hand on the nape of her neck and did a feline-type stretch of her back to try and ease the stress from her body.

Bryan has been gone for a year. With his declining health and medical needs, the physical part of their relationship had been over for more than three years.

She'd learned to live without marital affection or physical satisfaction. Truthfully, it had been the last thing on her mind. Being with Bryan was enough. More than enough.

But Bryan was gone.

And like it or not, she was still here. She thought back to Bryan's letters. Deep inside, she knew if Bryan could see her now he would be laughing and pushing her forward to move on with her life and be happy.

But as much as she wanted to accept Bryan's wishes, she couldn't shake her misgivings that maybe she was moving too fast.

She needed to stop these crazy thoughts. The timing was wrong. It might always be wrong. She was grieving. She shouldn't be feeling anything for anyone right now.

But someone should tell that to her body. It was responding almost without her control. Heartbeats thumping away at break neck speed at the mere sight of Michael. Heat washing through her body with a current like the rapids headed for the waterfall whenever she'd feel his eyes on her. Goosebumps slithering up and down her arms at the slightest touch of his hand.

As for her womanly parts...

The unused, long-thought-dead female parts sprang to life with a vengeance letting her know in no uncertain terms they were alive and well. The woman coming back to life wants to explore, taste, and tempt.

God, please help me.

If she didn't know better, she could have sworn she heard Bryan laughing. To heck with timing. He'd be right. Three years of chronic, serious illness and one year of grieving seemed to be enough time to move on. Right?

The tea kettle whistle startled her and interrupted her errant thoughts. She might not be able to control her body's reactions but she should certainly be adult enough to control her thoughts and actions. And she would. Right now. Right this minute. Michael is simply a nice man helping her set up a tree for the holidays. Period. She wasn't going to make more of it than it is.

She set out two mugs filled with boiling water and steeping tea bags onto a tray. She drew the cinnamon apple fragrance deeply into her lungs, released a long, slow breath and did it again, until she felt her shoulders relax and her tension waft away with the tea's steam.

On a whim, she also set out a small plate and filled it with homemade chocolate chip and sugar cookies. She wasn't trying to impress him. Heck, no. But being in the house alone for days had led her to bake...and bake...and bake some more. She couldn't feed the cookies to Pug.

She chuckled as she glanced at the dog and noted his obvious discomfort. He was pacing back and forth in the kitchen doorway. The poor, crazy mutt had a real dilemma on his hands, or should she say his paws, didn't he? He never appeared comfortable unless she was within sight, yet he still refused to come within arm's reach of her, and it was obvious he wanted to be in the thick of things watching Michael put the lights on the tree. The dilemma sent him scooting in circles.

"Karma doesn't feel good does it, Pug?" She laughed and picked up the tray. "Okay, let's go. We'll stay in the same room so you don't have to go crazy wondering which one of us to watch."

When she reached the den, the sight of the lit Christmas tree brought her to a dead stop. It looked so exquisite it almost didn't need ornaments. He'd done a wonderful job. She set down the tray and her eyes searched the room for Michael. She spotted him looking at photographs on the mantel. She crossed the room to join him.

"The tree looks beautiful, Michael. Thank you."

He turned toward her and shrugged. "All I did was set up some lights. No biggie." He gestured to the wedding photo she'd taken from the top of the television and placed on the mantel. "This is really a nice picture of the two of you. You look happy."

A bittersweet smile claimed her lips. "We were."

"And this one?" He pointed to a small 4x6 of the two of them covered from head to toe in whip cream. "This has to have an interesting story attached."

Eve chewed on her lower lip and tried to hold back a laugh. "Oh, there's a story, all right. I had taken a cake decorating class but, unfortunately, cake decorating doesn't seem to be one of my many talents." She stepped closer and stared at the picture. "Nobody could tell me that, of course. I was sure I was the best baker in the entire world. This particular evening I had a few female friends over to try out a new cake I was designing. It came out lopsided and..." she shrugged. "And ugly as sin."

She laughed. "One of my friends, Julie Marsh, one of my best friends actually, tried to suggest I try my hand at something other than cake decorating." She shook her head as the memory flooded back. "I took it as an insult, got mad and squirted her in the face with whip cream."

Michael's eyes widened and his mouth fell open. Then he shook his head and he chuckled.

"Yeah, I know," she said. "Not one of my finer moments."

Michael pointed to the photo. "And did your husband make the mistake of telling you the same thing?"

"You could say that." She stepped up for a closer view of the picture and laughed some more. "Bryan had been walking past the kitchen. He heard what was said and saw what I did. He got so upset. He marched into the room and told me I needed to apologize, immediately."

Michael glanced at the picture. "This picture tells me you didn't agree with him."

She shook her head. "Nope. I shot him in the face with whip cream."

Michael laughed. "And?"

"Bryan grabbed the can out of my hand and sprayed me from head to toe. I screamed, got another can, and sprayed him from head to toe." She grinned. "My friend, the one I had originally doused, took a picture of the two of us on her cell phone. She said she wanted to have a permanent record of what a jerk I could be." Her smile widened. "That was one of the reasons she was, and still is today, one of my very best friends. She calls things as they are and loves me anyway."

Michael stared at the picture for several seconds. When he looked back, his eyes darkened and the smile left his face. "From everything you've told me about your husband and looking at this picture, I feel pretty safe in saying, like your friend, he picked up on a fault or two you might have and loved you anyway."

Tears misted her eyes. She nodded. The silence, a quiet, companionable one, stretched between them as they both seemed lost in their own thoughts. After a few minutes, she touched his arm. "Come on, let's sit down. The tea is getting cold."

They sat next to each other, sipping tea, munching cookies, laughing, and swapping stories of Christmases past, of special spousal memories. It seemed natural, and even comfortable, to talk about Bryan with this man and she felt honored he felt he could share several memories he had of his wife with her. They did, indeed, share a unique bond. But from the tightening in her gut and the warmth flushing up her neck, Eve realized that initial bond was slowly turning into something else…something special…something new. She just wasn't sure she wanted it to.

When they'd finished their tea and cookies, Michael asked, "Mind if I help you with the rest of the decorations? My wife and I used to do them together but since I've moved back in with my parents, that job belongs to my mother and Katie. Anybody else is considered a trespasser."

Eve glanced at him and saw a dash of longing in his eyes. Their conversation about their spouses and past Christmases apparently raised some happy memories for both of them. He'd been so kind to her. How could she think of denying him the chance to relive one of his own?

"Well, if you're as good at hanging ornaments as you are at stringing lights, how can I say no? You already know the ornaments are in the box on the chair and the two boxes on the floor next to the chair. Help yourself."

Eve put on one of her favorite stations that played 24/7 holiday music and they spent the next hour trimming the tree. Sometimes she'd discreetly move an ornament from where he'd placed it to a spot she thought more suitable. Sometimes, he'd not-so-discreetly grab one of her placements and distribute it to a totally different branch. They laughed. They teased. And in no time the tree was trimmed from top to bottom.

Eve stood back admiring their work and relishing the comradery of the afternoon. "We did it. I truly think I have the best tree in the whole county this year."

"I agree. But it seems we forgot one."

She glanced over her shoulder.

Michael held up the gazebo ice skating ornament. "This is great. Working lights, too. Where did you find it?"

She accepted the ornament from his hand. "At the Old Christmas Shoppe on Main Street."

He stepped closer to her, the warmth of his breath tickling the back of her neck, the musky scent of his cologne mingling pleasantly with the tree's scent of evergreen. "It reminds me of the Sunday we went skating."

"Me, too. That's why I bought it. Every year Bryan and I would purchase one special ornament together for the tree. Something different. Something that had a personal memory attached to it." Her eyes moistened but she never lost the smile on her face. "This year...someone very close to me...suggested that I carry on the tradition this year on my own. Urged me to pick something special. Something fun." She shrugged. "When I saw this..."

Michael cupped her chin. His touch was surprisingly gentle for a man who worked outdoors for a living. He tilted her face until he was looking straight down into her eyes. "Thank you," he whispered, his voice husky. "I'm honored to think I was able to bring a little bit of happiness into your life during a time I know is anything but."

A little bit of happiness...

That's why Bryan had written her those letters. To help her through this holiday. To urge her to go on with her life, to be happy.

Michael lowered his head. Eve caught her breath.

Oh God! Oh God! He's going to kiss me.

And he did.

He pressed warm lips against her forehead. When he pulled back, he replaced his lips with his own forehead and looked into her eyes.

"It's time, Eve." Michael said.

"Time?" She sputtered the word. Her head spun and her heart thrashed so hard she was certain it would fly right out of her chest like a frightened bird who had been caged too long.

Michael grinned, stepped back and held out his hand. "We have to go shopping. We have a dog to find."

Eleven

More than two dozen cages held a wide variety of large, small, and in-between dogs of mixed breeds and various ages. Michael's ears rang with the shrill, ear-breaking sound of dog's loud, frantic barking and the pungent smell of animal no matter how hard the kennel workers tried to keep things clean. Each dog ran to the front of their kennel. If he didn't know better, he'd swear the dogs knew this was a potential chance for their freedom and not one of them wanted to be overlooked.

Michael hung back slightly and watched Eve as she moved from one dog to the next. She cooed and talked to each one. Her gentleness and obvious affection for the animals only endeared her to him more. He didn't need to ask. He was certain, if it was possible, she would adopt every one of them.

She looked back his way, her brow wrinkled and a frown pulling her lips almost into a grimace. "I don't know, Michael. It's so hard to choose. All of these dogs need good homes."

Yep, I'm right. She's nothing but a big softie.

"I know. I get it." He came up behind her and waited until he had her undivided attention. "Don't worry. Eve. This is a no-kill shelter. Eventually, every one of these dogs will be adopted, and they will be well cared for while they wait. That's why my family and I are large financial supporters of this particular shelter."

Her shoulders relaxed and a genuine smile lit her face. "Great to know. Now I don't feel like a traitor if I choose one dog over another."

Michael grinned. "Is that what was bothering you? I thought you were just being your usual Ms.-Can't-Decide self."

She huffed, stuck out the tip of her tongue, and gave him a playful shove.

He chuckled. He had to admit the tip of her tongue was as adorable as the rest of her. He had to work hard to subdue his sudden urge to pull her into his arms, kiss her deeply, and see if that tongue tasted as delectable as he imagined.

Despite the high-pitched barking, as well as standing in one of the most unromantic settings he could imagine, he was mesmerized by her. He wanted to touch her. Hold her. Run his fingers through her thick, long waves of auburn hair. He could barely take his eyes away from that perfectly shaped mouth that quietly invited his attention. Attention he was more than willing to give. Heat flowed throughout his entire body waking up areas he had largely ignored for years. He could tell from the flush creeping up Eve's throat and spreading in the cutest way across her cheeks that she felt the same way around him.

What are you doing, stupid? Trying to chase her away? You told her you wouldn't push. You promised to be her friend. Some friend. Good thing she can't read minds.

He lowered his eyes and coughed into a closed fist.

What he was starting to feel about Eve had little to do with friendship and it worried him. He'd met a couple of women over the years who became good friends, friends-with-benefits, and that scenario worked well for everyone. No expectations other than a pleasant evening and a mutual itch scratched. No family involvement. No commitments.

But with Eve…

Well, that scenario never entered his mind. She'd already met Katie and they got along great. She was already on the "come to dinner" mom list. Eve wasn't a friends-with-benefits consideration.

But did he really want to be starting a relationship at this stage of his life? Everything was going well. His parents helped out with Katie. He worked with his dad and brother. He had his occasional female friend. Everyone seemed happy and content. Why change things?

Because I can't get her out of my mind and she's slowly taking up residence in my heart. That's why.

She's not ready for a relationship he reminded himself. She's grieving. She's still wearing her wedding ring for Chris sake.

But that's not what is really gnawing at my gut, is it? I'm afraid. Maybe for the first time in my life really worried about taking a chance.

How could he possibly measure up to a man she'd loved her entire life? Especially a dead man she spoke about like he'd been a saint? A living, breathing man? Yeah, maybe he'd have a decent shot. But how the heck was he supposed to compete with a ghost?

I know. It isn't a competition. I get it.

These feelings, stirring inside him, in no way took away anything from the memories he had of his wife. But he'd taken off his ring and moved forward with his life years ago. As long as that wedding ring sat on Eve's finger and her eyes could mist with tears at the mere mention of the guy's name, he knew she wasn't ready for a new relationship...and maybe never would be. After all, they had experienced everything in life together. From kindergarten for heaven's sake. What did he have to offer?

He wasn't used to this sudden lack of confidence. It chewed at his gut and he didn't like it. He'd been shot down by women before. He'd dated throughout high school and college and had experienced his share of break-ups, too. It's a path to maturity. It's life and life goes on, right?

But the death of his wife had shattered his heart into a million pieces and damaged his soul. He couldn't look at life the same way, anymore. He appreciated the fragility of it...the fleetingness of time...the finality of it. Sure, he'd gotten back on his feet, went on with his life, and found a comfortable degree of contentment with his daughter and his family. But was he willing to expose the pieces of his taped-together heart to the possibility of being shattered again? Breaking this time because her husband's shadow would be too big for him to overcome?

No, he didn't need the complications. And he didn't want them.

But that was before a flying Pug and a beautiful human being named Eve literally fell into his life.

A mental image of the diamond wedding set on her left hand suddenly appeared like a 3-D movie in his mind. This woman's heart is already taken. He'd be setting himself up for guaranteed heartbreak and he didn't dare risk losing any more pieces of himself.

He glanced up. When he saw the quizzical expression on her face, he wondered how long he'd been standing there musing about things that needed no debate.

"So?" he smiled. "Any doggie candidates?"

She grinned and then moved down two cages. "I'd like to see this one." She pointed to a small mixed breed, and mixed it was. The ears stood up and appeared much too large for the dog's tiny head. It had a barrel chest, tiny legs, and wiry black fur sticking up and out every which way like someone had thrown the dog into a clothes dryer without fabric softener.

"That one?" Michael took a quick glance around at the dogs in the other cages. He saw pit bulls, labs, hounds, a couple of German shepherd mixes, even a little, adorable dachshund. Any one of these dogs looked better than the one Eve picked. "Are you sure?" he asked, not able to disguise his doubt.

"Look at her eyes, Michael. She has the most beautiful dark brown eyes. They almost look like black buttons."

"She?"

Eve pointed to the card hanging on the cage door. "Her name is Bella."

Michael stood behind Eve as she squatted down and poked her fingers through the cage trying to pet the animal. "Okay, her eyes are cute. But have you taken a good look at the rest of her?"

"Michael!" She shot up and gave him a disapproving look. "Shame on you. She's adorable. The word Bella means beautiful and I think the name suits her."

Michael took a good long look at the small dog in the cage and laughed out loud. "Are you and I looking at the same dog?"

Eve stood her ground and sent him a challenging glare. "Beauty isn't only skin deep, Michael. There is a loving, sweet aura coming off this dog. She's housebroken. Friendly. The card says she's three-years-old so she's puppy-like without needing the intense care a puppy would need. I'd like to take her out in the yard for a bit to get to know her a little better and be sure. But I think this might be the perfect pet for Katie." She shrugged her shoulders. "You asked for my opinion and I'm giving it to you. But this is your gift to your daughter and the final decision is yours."

He took another look at the dog and tried to figure out what kind of breed it might be. Part French Bull dog, for sure, with those ears and chest. Definitely terrier of some kind. As for the tiny legs and tiny head, only the Lord knows what else got stirred in the mix. Whatever it was, this poor dog had definitely inherited the worst of all of its gene pool.

He'd bet it could win one of those ugly dog contests he'd seen advertised on cable television. He studied the dog for a minute more. He couldn't believe it but there was something about the little squirt that kept his attention. He sort of liked this little creature.

"She isn't ugly, Michael. She's precious and adorable," Eve said.

As if on cue, the tiny animal stood on her hind legs, supporting her body with her front paws against the cage. Those small button eyes locked on him and didn't move, her back end and her tail wiggling away. She might be an ugly dog but she was a smart one. Obviously, she knew he would be the one she'd have to convince. He glanced back and forth between the two females staring at him, and laughed.

"You know what? I think maybe this kind of ugly is starting to grow on me."

Eve's face burst into the brightest smile, while the dog continued to wiggle and waggle away for his attention. He held up his hands. "Okay, I give up." He gestured to one of the attendants. "Can we take this one out into the yard, please?"

"Sure thing." The attendant opened the cage, tethered the animal, and handed the leash to Eve.

Once outside the dog went nuts. It looked like a cartoon animal that had its first taste of freedom. Bella raced in circles totally twisting the leash. She'd stop for a quick lick on Eve's shoe, ankle, and leg, anything she could reach. And she was smart enough to cover all bases by doing the same for his shoes and lower leg. Then she stood up on her hind legs and pawed the air. Falling back to earth, she rolled on her back on the grass, and then flopped her body back and forth begging for a belly rub.

"See." Eve laughed and then squatted down and lovingly rubbed the little dog's belly. "Isn't she perfect?"

Now that Eve was in a lowered position, Bella made her move. She twisted back around to her feet, jumped into Eve's arms, and showered her face with dozens of doggie kisses. Eve collapsed in a spasm of laughs and cuddled the dog closer.

"Are you sure this is the one? I thought we were here to find a dog that hated you," Michael teased.

She totally ignored the barb and cuddled the dog closer, rubbing her face in the dog's fur.

He gazed down at Eve's flushed face, her sparkling eyes, her wide grin, and his gut took a definite hit.

"Her name suits her, don't you think?" Eve grinned. "Isn't she beautiful?"

Michael smiled down at this enchanting woman who, if he wasn't careful, had the power to seize his heart and hold it the palm of her hand, seemingly without her even knowing it.

"She certainly is," he whispered, knowing he wasn't talking about the dog at all.

Twelve

"Wait a minute, Mom. I can't hear you." Eve scooted both Bella and Pug into the garage and shut the door. "Sorry about that. Now, what did you say?" She grabbed her brewed tea, black tea this time. She'd need fortification for this call, for sure. "No, you're right, that didn't sound like Pug because it wasn't Pug. Don't get excited. I didn't get another dog. Not exactly." She took a quick sip of her tea while she listened to the litany of questions coming from her mom's end of the telephone call.

"A friend of mine adopted a dog for his daughter for Christmas so I'm doggie-sitting until Santa can deliver his gift. No, I don't think that was a lot to ask. Michael has done plenty for me. He helped me pick out a Christmas tree, delivered it, put up the lights, even helped decorate it. The least I could do is return the favor and help him out by watching this dog for him." She rolled her eyes at her mother's protests. "Mom, the distraction is exactly what I need. I thought you didn't want me sitting here all alone feeling sorry for myself."

Eve had to chuckle as her mother back-paddled and reminded her how she tried to take her with her to Florida for the holidays. "No, I'm not sitting her feeling sorry for myself. And the dog is not a problem. The dog is adorable. It's only for ten more days. Piece of cake."

She breathed in the cinnamon apple scent and took a bigger gulp of the brew. "Yes, Mom, Michael belongs to *that* McGruder family. I mentioned him to you before. He's the man Pug jumped on and stole his sandwich. Yes, the same man. He's the widower with the four-year-old daughter I told you about." Eve took a deep breath and spoke quickly, trying to beat her mother to the pass. "Look, don't you get all worked up and start reading anything into it. We're friends. Period."

Eve's memories flashed to childhood when her mom read her the story of Pinocchio. She couldn't help but wonder if her nose had just grown another inch or two.

"Mom, don't I hear Connie calling you? No, really, I think you should check. Maybe she wants to take you someplace fun. Yes, I'll call you in a couple of days. I love you, too, Mom. Bye."

She chuckled. Well, she'd survived her mother's first round of interrogations unscathed. And she knew there'd be plenty more to come. But moms will be moms. Eve sat back and let out a heavy sigh.

We're just friends, Mom.

Eve couldn't resist. She reached up and touched the end of her nose.

Eve pulled her Honda Fit up in front of the McGruder house, cut the engine, but didn't get out of the car. She stared at the festive Christmas lights outlining the house, the porch, and edging the front entrance. A large, evergreen wreath, covered with an equally large red bow, adorned the front door. The entire scene was warm, welcoming, and definitely filled with holiday spirit.

She tapped her fingers on the steering wheel and took several deep breaths.

Why did you accept Ruth's dinner invitation?

She leaned back and stared out the windshield into the night sky.

Because it was the polite thing to do after turning down her former invitation. Because I enjoyed spending time with this lovely family and I'd like to get to know them better. And because I've been sitting alone in the house for the last two days talking to a dog. Time to get out, see real people, have fun.

She twisted her fingers around the car key but didn't pull it out of the ignition.

Yeah, right. I can't even be honest with myself. It's only been two days since I've seen Michael...and I miss him.

"Grrrr." She slammed the palm of her hand against the steering wheel. "Go home, Eve. You don't belong here," she shouted into empty air.

Yet, she made no move to follow her own directions despite the wave of guilt having a field day in her mind right now. She didn't want to be thinking about any man right now. She was grieving the loss of her husband. And it shouldn't matter that a part of her would always grieve for Bryan. She just knew she wasn't supposed to be attracted to another man or be dealing with the feelings she felt every time she was him.

Because?

Because her husband has only been dead a year. It's too soon for her to even look at another man, let alone be developing feelings for one.

Michael is dead. I can scream and swear and pound my fist in the air and he will still be dead. He'd been gravely ill for three years. He's been physically gone for an additional year. He'd be the first one to tell you it was time to move on and start living your life. Matter of fact, he did. Maybe twenty times is the magic number.

As if she hadn't re-read them every day and every night since she'd found them. Maybe it was time to truly listen to his words.

Eve turned her head and took a slow, long look at the front door. She could almost imagine the scene inside. Mrs. McGruder scurrying around the kitchen checking on last minute details. Mr. McGruder, probably in the living room with his feet propped up on an ottoman, waiting to be called to supper. Katie under everyone's feet, a bundle of energy and curiosity. And Michael...

Feelings forming for Michael? Really?

Images of Michael flashed through her mind. The astonishment and humor on his face when Pug had jumped in his lap. Sharing soft pretzels on a cold winter night. Seeing him grin at her from behind the collection table at church. His patience and good conversation as they walked his farm to pick out a tree. The vulnerability flashing across his face when he trusted her enough to share stories of his wife and their life together. And his willingness to listen to her memories, too. The fun of decorating the tree together—the teasing, the comradery. And, of course, Bella. He'd listened. Resisted. Then melted. Yeah, he was a really special guy.

Eve couldn't believe where her thoughts were dragging her heart. She was a thirty-five-year-old woman who had never been attracted to another man, never dated anyone else even in school. Bryan was her knight in shining armor from kindergarten to grave. She'd loved him...deeply...probably from the first day in kindergarten...and she knew a piece of her heart always would.

And that didn't mean she was foolish enough to think she'd have to stay celibate the rest of her life at her age. That's just stupid. She's a woman and, eventually, will want to be with a man, again. Probably thanks to Bryan. He'd made marriage a safe place, a true partnership, full of love and surprises and laughs. Of course, she'd want that back in her life again.

But now?

Was she really thinking of beginning a relationship before she was certain she had truly said good-bye to the last one? Of course, not.

But Michael...

No question this man affected her. His intellect engaged her mind. His kindness and thoughtfulness touched her heart. And physically even the slightest grazing of his hand on her body made her want to jump out of her skin. She didn't know how to be around another man...to be *with* another man...and she was scared, so scared where these feelings were taking her.

She leaned her forehead on her hands resting on the top of the steering wheel.

Bryan, help me. What should I do? I feel so guilty, like somehow I'm betraying you. But I also can't deny that I enjoy being around Michael. I really think you would like him. He's a good, decent, kind man. He's intelligent, funny, a great dad...and he's lost his wife, too. He understands the pain and the grief that never fully goes away. He's lived it. Tears misted her eyes. *Bryan. Bryan. My dearest, dearest Bryan. I've never needed to talk to my best friend more than I do right now. But you're not here.*

"Eve?"

Startled, she raised her head and watched as Michael, who had been standing in an open doorway, pulled the door shut behind him and made his way to the driver's side of her car. He twirled his fingers indicating she lower her window, which she did.

"Hi, you," he said.

His smile warmed her heart, among other parts of her anatomy. She looked at the crinkled the skin beside his eyes and then gazed into those gorgeous deep blue eyes. She fought the urge to reach out and stroke his cheek which was already showing signs of a five o'clock shadow.

He placed his forearms on the open window ledge and leaned his head close. "Everything okay? You've been sitting out here for a while."

Her heart hiccupped then settled into a steady, strong beat. Suddenly, a calmness spread over her entire body and she truly believed she was getting her answer…from the very best friend she had ever had. She shot her eyes skyward for just a second before smiling at the man standing in front of her.

"Hello, Michael. Everything's fine."

"Good." He opened the car door, offered his hand and helped her out. "Everyone is inside, hungry, and waiting for you."

She chuckled. "Well, we can't keep hungry people waiting now, can we?" She looped her hand through his arm as they made their way into the house.

"Miss Eve!" Katie came flying down the hall, skidded across the foyer in her stocking feet, and wrapped her little arms around Eve's hips giving her the biggest hug a four-year-old could give. When she let her go, the child looked behind her. "Did you bring Pug?"

"Not this time, honey."

Michael helped Eve out of her coat and took her gloves.

"Why didn't Pug come? I would have shared my dinner with him."

Eve chuckled. "Because Pug is babysitting tonight." She threw an accusing glance Michael's way. "He's got a new friend that is staying with us for a little while." She placed a hand on the girl's shoulder. "I'll make sure to bring him by and let you get some play time with him real soon."

"Promise?"

Eve crossed her heart with her fingers. "Promise."

Ruth joined them in the foyer. "Hello, dear. You're just in time. My homemade biscuits just came out of the oven and dinner is ready. Can I interest you in a glass of wine?"

"Wine would be lovely, thank you."

"White or red?"

"White, please."

Michael placed his hand on Eve's waist and gently steered her behind Ruth and Katie toward the dining room. "Don't let her fool you," he whispered in her ear, his warm breath raising goosebumps on her flesh. "She's going to put on a lavish spread but pretend that it wasn't any big deal to prepare. Take it from me, she's been cooking and baking all day and definitely wants this night to be perfect."

Eve turned her head, her lips only inches away from his. Their breath mingled for a single heartbeat. "It already is."

His eyes darkened, his expression sobered, and for one brief moment she thought he was struggling not to kiss her. The thought that he might be as unsure of their budding relationship as she was made her smile.

"What?" he asked.

"Nothing," she said, leaning a little closer to him and looked up into his face. "I'm just glad I'm here."

"Me, too."

For just a second, Eve could have sworn she saw unbridled desire in his eyes, just a flash, and then it was gone like he'd purposely flipped a switch. He grinned and continued to lead her into the dining room.

"Ms. Eve, you can sit next to me. I saved you a seat." Katie patted the chair beside her.

"Thank you, Katie, I'd love to." Eve took the seat offered and smiled down at Katie sitting to her right. She was pleased but not surprised when Michael claimed the chair to her left. Seth and Ruth took their seats at opposite ends of the table. Danny, accompanied by his own female friend, Jane, made introductions and then settled in opposite her.

Pot roast moist enough to slice with a fork, tender vegetables, salad, and homemade yeast rolls decorated the table and filled the air with a delectable aroma. Eve, swallowing any pretense of shyness or good manners, enjoyed every bite and dived in for seconds of everything. Shamefully, she actually considered squeezing in a third helping. Everything was so delicious, but she'd spotted homemade pies resting on the buffet and she knew she had to save room for pie.

The grin on her face was non-stop, almost to the point of her face hurting. Not just for the wonderful meal but for the entertaining company. The conversations around the table bounced like ping-pong balls from one subject to the next, some conversations light, some intense, some downright hysterical. She couldn't remember the last time she'd laughed so hard or had so much fun.

She stood and helped Ruth clear the dishes while Sean McGruder doled out slices of pie for all. Michael made sure no coffee cup went unattended. Danny and Jane volunteered for final clean-up. Everyone laughing. Everyone talking. Everyone celebrating family and friends.

Yep. This night was turning out exactly as she said. Perfect.

Thirteen

Eve bent down and loaded the last dish in the dishwasher.

"Thank you for the help, Eve. But I told you it really wasn't necessary. You're our guest." Ruth appeared in front of her, drying her hands on a dish towel and grinning like a Cheshire cat.

Eve straightened. "It's no trouble, Ruth. It's the least I can do to say thank you for such a wonderful meal. Since it's just Pug and I, I don't cook much, anymore. If I can't heat it, nuke it in the microwave, or fry it on the stove top, I'm not interested."

Both women chuckled.

"I understand, dear." Ruth closed the dishwasher, then gently grasped Eve's elbow. "Now that we have a few minutes alone, I was wondering if we could talk."

Apprehension climbed up Eve's back bone, but she smiled, nodded and allowed herself to be led to a seat at the kitchen table as far away from the dining room as they could get. Eve folded her hands on the table and waited. The older woman sat down opposite her, leaned forward and placed a hand on top of hers. "I wonder if I can ask you to do me a favor. A huge favor, I know. But I really hope you say yes."

"With a build up like that I'm almost afraid to ask what it is." Eve smiled but shifted uncomfortably. Something was up. She couldn't help feeling she was about to be ambushed.

Ruth released her hand and leaned back in her chair. "There's only seven days left until Christmas."

"I've heard that rumor." She shot the older woman a quizzical look and waited for the other shoe to drop.

"And tomorrow's Sunday."

The look of worry on Ruth's face almost made Eve laugh out loud.

"Yes, Ruth, tomorrow is definitely Sunday, seven days until Christmas. And????" She felt like she was volleying one of her mother's fifty-question telephone calls. She wondered if all mothers do this.

Ruth came straight to the point and spoke quickly. "I'm the chairwoman for the Women's Guild. We rented the church hall for our annual community Christmas party. All of the children, particularly ones from neighborhoods where Christmas rarely comes, look forward to the event. They get a hot meal, talk with Santa, and every single child goes home with a Christmas present."

Ruth's serious tone caught and held her attention while she waited for the woman to take a deep breath and continue.

"And I need your help." Ruth's words rushed out in a gush of air.

"Me? Of course, I'd be glad to help. But I'm not exactly sure what you want me to do. Do you need me to buy a gift for a child or provide transportation or serve snacks?" She smiled broadly. "Tell me you need Christmas cookies. I've got dozens already made and ready to go."

"No, dear." Ruth waved away her suggestions. "We have all of that covered."

"Okay, then what's this huge favor?" She raised an eyebrow and studied the older woman.

"I need you to be our elf."

"Elf?" Eve fell back in her chair, her eyes widened, her mouth fell open. She couldn't have been more surprised at the ridiculous request. "Me? An elf? I can't be an elf."

"Please, Eve. I see how you are with Katie. You're great with children. You'd be a perfect elf."

Eve overcame her surprise and started to laugh out loud. "Ruth, I'm not elf material, believe me."

"Oh please, Eve. Mackenzie Brubecker is sick and had to cancel at the last minute. The event is tomorrow. There's no time to find another elf at this late date."

"Ruth, I appreciate that you have a problem but I'm not your answer. I'd make a terrible elf. Trust me." Seeing her disappointment, Eve continued, "I'm sure one of the other ladies in your women's guild could fill in for Mackenzie. You don't need me."

Ruth got up, grabbed a bag from the pantry, and hurried back to her seat.

Eve eyed the bag and realized she'd walked into a well-prepared trap.

"I'm afraid my fellow guild members are long past the years when they can fit into this outfit." Ruth tossed the bag on the table. "And even if one of the more trim ladies wanted to give it a try, she'd look ridiculous at our age in sheer green tights."

"Green tights?" A sense of dread began to creep up her spine.

She watched Ruth pull out the sheerest green leotards she's ever seen, as well as a vest that wasn't long enough to cover up much, a hat, and fake pointy ears.

"Oh-h-h-h." Eve felt like a mouse in a trap that was just about to snap down on her.

Eve picked up the leotard and gazed in shock at the fake ears, vest, and hat. "No. No," she sputtered, lowering the material to the table and leaning back in her chair and chuckled. "I'd do a lot of things to help you out, Ruth. But I'm not elf material. Trust me. I fall over my own feet, let alone try to walk around in these." She lifted the slippers with the curled up toes.

Ruth remained silent.

Eve hated to see the crestfallen expression on the woman's face.

Don't look at me like that. I'm carrying plenty of guilt already, I don't need more.

"What's one elf?" Eve asked. "It sounds like it's going to be a wonderful party. Food. Gifts. Santa." She shrugged her shoulders. "What's one little elf? I bet no one will even miss the elf."

Ruth's mouth formed a perfect little circle. "You don't understand, dear. We need our elf. The elf leads the children, one at a time, up to the stage to sit on Santa's lap. The elf takes pictures of the kids with Santa. The elf entertains the kids standing in line waiting. The elf is super important. We definitely need an elf." The woman almost looked like she was going to cry. "Please, Eve. I told you it would be a big favor. And it is. But it's for the children. For some of them, it will be the only Christmas, the only gift they will get."

If she didn't know better, she could have sworn she heard Bryan laughing his head off. This is exactly the type of ambush he would have loved. And for a cause he would have loved, too. Eve sighed heavily. She knew when she was defeated. She smiled as the thought crossed her mind that Michael might have felt just as pressured and blind-sided when she'd pressed him to adopt Bella. She gathered the material on the table and held out her hand for the bag. "What time do I have to be there?"

The older woman squealed with delight and clapped her hands together. "Thank you, Eve. You're doing a wonderful thing for the children. Don't worry, dear, you'll make a perfect elf."

Eve slid the outfit into the brown paper bag and smiled.

Yep. I can cross this off my bucket list. Always wanted to be an elf.

The sound of Bryan's laughter echoed through her head.

Eve studied her reflection in the floor length mirror. She had to admit the costume fit her like a glove, a tight glove, but a glove. Everything that needed covering was covered. The tips on he elf shoes were a little much. Clodhoppers in disguise. She leaned in and took a long, hard look at the ears. She wanted to make sure they were on securely and wouldn't fall off in front of a child and scar them for life.

She caught a glimpse of Pug in her peripheral vision. The dog had been coming into the rooms lately, still staying an arm's length away, but definitely no longer watching from the doorway. Bella, Pug's constant shadow, followed close behind. Both dogs sat staring at her and, if she didn't know better, she could swear that was an ear-to-ear grin on Pug's face.

"Okay, I get it. Elf ears and reindeer ears. Not funny." She laughed and held up the reindeer ears and looked down at Pug. "But Bryan asked for the reindeer ears this year, buddy, so live with it. Reindeer ears for you. Elf ears for me. And both of us making kids happy. Right?"

She snatched the ears off the night table and attached them to Pug's head. The dog made a half-hearted swipe at them with his paw but seemed to accept the inevitable and left them in place. Eve laughed as she imagined the pleasure Bryan was having if he could see his reindeer dog and elf wife.

"As for you, Ms. Bella, I have to put you in your kennel for a few hours. Sorry." She scooted the dog inside. "I know you want to come but that would spoil Katie's Christmas surprise. We can't have that now, can we?" She gave the dog a final pat and threw both a chew toy and doggie treat inside. "It won't be that long, I promise."

Eve grabbed her cell phone on its second ring, listened for a second, and then responded. "Hi, Mom. Good to hear from you but I can't talk long, I'm on my way out." She shooed Pug out of the room. "I'm playing an elf for the children's party the Women's Guild is putting on." She walked to the kitchen knowing Pug would be close behind. When she reached the door to the garage she called Pug. She attached his leash and straightened his reindeer ear. She patted his head and was surprised that for the first time in the last year he didn't move away. Still puzzling over Pug's new behavior, she turned her attention back to the conversation with her mother.

"Yes, you heard right. It's no big deal. Ruth asked me to fill in because her original elf called in sick at the last minute."

Eve rolled her eyes. "I'm simply helping out a friend. Yes, you could say I've become friends with the entire family. What? No, I'm not expecting Michael to be there. Why would he be attending a Women's Guild event? Mom...please." She picked up her purse, grabbed Pug's leash, and let herself into the garage.

"Yes, I had a good time at dinner last night. Ruth gave me her recipe for her pot roast. The gravy alone was superb, and the meat was so tender you could cut it with a fork. I even twisted her arm for the special ingredient that made her homemade apple pie, one of the best I have ever tasted." Eve chuckled. "Don't worry, you'll get a chance to meet her when you get back from Florida. If you're lucky, I'll try my hand at cooking the same meal and invite the entire family over. How about that?"

She listened to the life events on her mother's end as she lifted Pug into the car and buckled him in. "Yep. Seven days until Christmas." She listened for a few more minutes and heard the words her mother wasn't saying. She heard the worry in her tone as she spoke of other things. She took note at how she purposely didn't ask about how Eve would weather Christmas morning alone or, worse, how she'd survive the first year anniversary of Bryan's death. But the questions hung in the air nonetheless.

"I'm fine, Mom. Really. Please, enjoy your holiday and don't worry about me." She slid into the driver's seat. "Of course, I'm going to call you Christmas morning. We'll do Facetime with the whole family, and I can watch my nieces open their gifts. Yes, I promise. Gotta run now, Mom. Elves can't be late." She made a kissing sound and hung up.

She had to admit that she wasn't sure, herself, how she'd feel this first Christmas alone. She'd never been alone. If she was honest, she wouldn't really be alone this year, either. She'd definitely get up early and do Facetime with her Florida family. That would be fun. And Michael would be bringing Katie over to meet Bella and take her home.

Then, life would return to normal, just her and Pug.

She glanced over at Pug and wondered if he'd hold Bella's departure against her like he had Bryan's. Poor Pug. Every time he gave his heart away, he got it broken. She reached out and pet the dog. Surprisingly, for the second time today, he didn't move away.

One lesson Eve had learned during the past three years, and had to remind herself occasionally, was to be here now. Don't worry about tomorrow. Don't dwell on the past. Or, she might miss those extra special moments forming memories today.

She turned the key in the ignition and backed out of the driveway.

Heigh ho, heigh ho, an elf and reindeer on the go!

Fourteen

"Eve, over here." Ruth beckoned to her from her position by a serving table. "You look wonderful! I knew you would. Turn around. Let me get a good look."

Eve's face filled with heat. "That's okay. Let's not and say we did."

Ruth laughed. "I understand. But you have nothing to be embarrassed about. The costume fits you perfectly. You're adorable."

"I left adorable behind in my teens, Ruth. I'm a grown woman squeezed into a costume a teenager should be wearing and we both know it."

Before Ruth could reply, two other older women rushed over and began gushing over her.

"You're right, Ruth." The first woman eyed her up and down. "Hi, I'm Marge. Thank you so much for saving us. We don't know what we would have done without our elf. And you do, indeed, make a perfect elf."

"The children are going to love you." The second woman introduced herself, "I'm Betty. My main job will be food prep and serving, but I'll also be helping you keep the kids entertained while they wait to see Santa."

Eve smiled and acknowledged both women. They exchanged pleasantries for a few minutes when Ruth cupped her elbow and started to pull her away. "Come, dear. The door will be opening any minute now. I have to show you where to stand and what to do."

Eve said good-bye to the other women and followed Ruth's lead. Ruth showed her where to stand to welcome the children, where to stand to take pictures, and showed her how to use the Women's Guild camera. She'd barely had time to ask a question or two when a wide, beaming smile lit the older woman's face, and she leaned forward and whispered, "Doors open. Here we go. Good luck!" Ruth stepped a foot or two away, and pointed to a container on the end of the nearest table. "I forgot to tell you. Give each child a candy cane after they've had their chance to talk with Santa, but remind them they aren't to open it until after dinner."

"Tell a child not to eat candy? Think they'll listen?"

Ruth grinned. "They will if you tell them Santa will be watching. Then, they will have to decide if they want their names put on the Good List or the Naughty List."

Eve laughed. She placed a small doggie bed on the floor and tied Pug's leash to the table leg. She'd extended the leash with a piece of cord so Pug would be able to move around without getting into trouble. Pug plopped into his doggie bed. He sat quietly, like a little angel, and waited to see what was going to happen next. If she didn't know better, she'd believe Pug knew what was expected of him and was waiting for the children to come over and pet him.

Pug didn't have long to wait. Once the doors opened, it was like a stampede. Children appeared everywhere. Betty and Ruth herded them into a straight line and explained to the kids what to expect. Then, pointed toward Pug and promised each child the opportunity to pet the "reindeer" dog. The kids didn't need any further motivation and formed in line with little coaxing.

The rustle of material sounded behind her. A quick glance told her Santa had arrived and Eve watched as he took his seat on his throne. Ruth nodded her way and Eve knew that was her signal to accompany the first child up to the stage to sit on Santa's lap. Once she had, she grabbed the camera, crossed to her spot, looked through the lens, and froze.

Michael.

She'd recognize those gorgeous sapphire eyes anywhere.

What was he doing here? How on earth had Ruth hoodwinked him into playing Santa?

Eve looked back into the camera lens, then, snapped the picture of the little boy on Santa's lap. But not before she noticed Santa direct a not-so-innocent-looking smile her way and then he winked.

The hours passed in a flurry of children's laughter, finger foods, tons of introductions to other members of the guild, church members, parents who stopped by to thank her for her participation in the event. She knew she'd never remember everyone's name, but she did her best to remember their faces. Surprisingly, she'd had a lot of fun. She'd remember this event, maybe even volunteer to help next year—but not as an elf.

It had been a long day, and even though the elf shoes had been comfortable, she still couldn't wait to get home, let Bella out of her kennel, put her feet up, and enjoy her beautiful, perfectly decorated Christmas tree.

Michael saw Eve getting ready to leave and hurried over. "Penny for your thoughts," he said.

Eve smiled. "Hello, Santa. I must admit I was surprised to see you, here."

Now that all the families, and even most of the workers had left, Michael removed his Santa beard. "Normally, I wouldn't be. This gig usually belongs to my dad."

"How did you get roped into it? I wouldn't think having almost a hundred children sit on your lap and recite their Christmas lists is something you'd volunteer to do."

"Have you met my mother, Ms. Elf?" he asked.

Probably with similar tactics she'd used on her. Ruth was pretty good at showing a sad face and stressing how it was for the good of the children.

But what about Katie? Wasn't Ruth or Michael afraid she'd recognize him and that would spoil Christmas this year?

Her eyes darted over each child in line and Eve realized Katie wasn't to be found. She probably should have already known. If Katie had come, she would have descended on reindeer Pug the moment she saw him. She was probably at home with Sean. Eve gave a sigh of relief,

"Point taken." Her smile widened.

She really had no idea how beautiful she was, especially when she smiled. An animation filled her expression, lit her eyes, and lightened her features. For one instant of insanity, he found himself wanting to make it his life's work to bring that happiness to her face—always.

"She was right, you know." He took his time moving his eyes over her body, letting his gaze caress her feminine curves, even if it was something he wouldn't allow his hands to do. The tell-tale flush that crept up her throat and reddened her cheeks, let him know his attention had not gone unnoticed. "I can't imagine anyone better suited to wear that costume."

She dropped her eyes, her flush darkened, and her reaction made his blood race through his veins like a dam bursting inside. She might have been married for thirteen years but she carried an aura of naiveté with her—and it only drew him to her, more. She admitted she hadn't been with anyone besides Bryan. Her slight shyness and awkwardness brought out his protective side. He had to keep reminding himself to hold back, take things slow, wait, even though every muscle in his body protested. But he knew, without a doubt she would be worth the wait.

"This isn't something I would normally volunteer to do but I have to admit I had fun," she said, her words riding on a husky whisper letting him know he was right in his assessment that he was having an effect on her.

This?

Oh, she wasn't talking about *this*…this invisible pull between them, this unspoken draw that neither of them wanted to admit feeling yet neither could deny. Okay. If she needed a change in subject, he would try to pretend the earth wasn't moving between them.

"Me, too," he said. "The look on their faces when I handed out the gifts was priceless. It felt good to make this a happy holiday for many of them. We both know life can be hard, and sometimes very unkind." He reached out and ran the pad of his thumb down her cheek. Her skin felt like silk and he wanted to touch more. "But everyone deserves to have at least one happy Christmas day."

He moved closer, only inches between them, and he could almost see her hold her breath. "If I can do that…provide even a little piece bit of happiness for someone…then that's what I want to do."

Eve's eyes widened and she looked like a deer frozen in headlights.

What the hell are you doing? He asked himself. *Whatever happened to slow and easy? What happened to being her friend and leaving your libido out of it?*

But he couldn't. His libido was doing its best to take charge and steer the ship.

He squeezed his eyes shut for a second and fought to bring his emotions, and his body, under control. Dinner. Let's bring the conversation back to dinner. That should be a safe subject.

"I'm glad you came to dinner last night," he said, not able to meet her eyes for fear she'd see his unbridled desire.

Small talk. Stick with small talk.

"I enjoyed sharing my family time with you. I don't normally bring friends home during the holidays."

Or ever, idiot. You never bring friends-with-benefits into your home. Ever. But Eve isn't in the friends-with-benefits category, is she? She holds a special place. She's in this-woman-can-break-your-heart category, remember?

"I'm glad you did, Michael. You have a wonderful family. I enjoyed every minute of the evening. The food, the conversation, the company. All of it."

"Good." He took a couple of steps back.

"Just think," Eve teased. "If I hadn't gone, then your mom wouldn't have had the chance to volunteer me for Ms. Elf today."

Michael chuckled. "Yeah, sorry about that."

"I'm not."

There was something in her tone of voice that made him look up— a huskiness, a damn perfect sexiness.

Then Eve did the last thing on earth he expected. She rushed forward almost as if she hesitated she might change her mind. Her arms reached up and her fingers wound themselves through the back of his hair. The touch of her skin against the nape of his neck seared his already aroused body with heat. She stood up on her toes, smiled directly into his eyes, and kissed him.

Fifteen

His lips were full, soft, a warm place to land when Eve pressed them against her own. She meant it to be a quick kiss but her body rebelled and wanted more, much more. His arms slid around her waist and pulled her close. Her body flush against him, she could feel his arousal and a little bit of female pride tempted her to try for more. He wanted her. Desired her. This plain, thirty-something book editor had made this devilishly handsome bachelor desire her.

He kissed her back, probing not just the depths of her mouth, but reaching to the depths of her soul.

What is it about this man? I'm so drawn. So entranced. So confused.

When their kiss ended, he continued to hold her close and smiled down into her eyes. "Aren't you a woman of many surprises? Pug must have learned his stealth approach from you." He chuckled one second before his head descended and he kissed her again.

Strongly. Passionately.

So that's where that term toe curling comes from?

This time when the kiss ended, she gently pulled out of his embrace. "Michael…"

He shot her a quizzical look but remained silent.

"Mistletoe," she whispered. Eve pointed over his left shoulder to a small sprig hanging from the archway. "You were standing under the mistletoe. I wanted to thank you for today…and for last night…and for…everything…" She wondered if her sudden wave of panic could be seen in her eyes. "I thought a quick kiss…"

Michael's back stiffened. A hooded look came over his eyes. "Mistletoe. Of course, what was I thinking? You wanted to plant a quick kiss under the mistletoe as a Christmas thank you."

She nodded.

"An innocent kiss between friends." Michael's eyes challenged her. She nodded again, slower this time.

His arms reached out and pulled her into his embrace. His eyes glittered with passion. The warmth of his breath brushed across her face as she breathed in the scent of candy cane and mint. "And the rest of the kiss?" he asked. "The deeper, passionate kiss. That was anything but a kiss between friends, Eve."

"I'm sorry if you mistook…"

"I didn't mistake anything, and if you'd be honest with yourself, you'd admit it," he insisted. "There's something special developing between us. Something deeper than friendship. We're beginning a relationship that for both of us is new and, I admit, can be a bit scary given our backgrounds."

Eve started to pull back but he clasped her elbows and stopped her.

"Be honest with me, Eve." His voice was husky with emotion. "Be honest with yourself. Don't you want to see where this new relationship can take us?"

His lips descended again and she was lost. He claimed her mouth, parried with her tongue, tasted, probed, explored, each of their breaths mingling with each other until it became one breath, their united breath. The kiss held such passion Eve thought her legs would collapse out from under her. She found herself leaning into him. Clutching his suit in her fists. Shivers raced down her spine and her entire body trembled. She couldn't breathe, could barely move.

"Talk to me, Eve," his lips whispered against her mouth. "Tell me I'm not wrong. Tell me you are feeling the same things I do." Michael's gaze froze her in place and demanded an answer.

"Michael…" She reached up and cupped the side of his face. When she did, the overhead light hit the diamond on her hand, causing a glint that caught both their attentions.

Slowly, Michael reached up and moved her fingers off his face. He held her hand between them, both of them staring at the diamond wedding set.

When she raised her eyes to look at him, she knew they were glistening with tears.

A bittersweet smile appeared on his lips and sadness lit his eyes. He placed an index finger against her lips when she started to speak. "Don't," he said. "I understand. It's okay. I don't want you to do anything or change anything for me. I want you to be you. Moving ahead at your own speed and in your own direction."

He reached out and softly touched the side of her face. His gaze locked with hers. "I believe we already have a special connection. I believe it can become something more, something real and lasting." He shrugged. "I'd like to see."

He slid a hand up and down her arm. "Believe me, I didn't want to have these feelings. Giving your heart to someone makes you vulnerable, makes it possible to be hurt. My heart was shattered once and it took me a long time to put the pieces together. I didn't plan on giving anyone a chance to shatter those pieces, again."

He gave a mirthless chuckle. "But I've got no choice. I finally realize I've already put my heart out there."

He cupped her chin and then kissed her lips softly, gently. When he looked into her eyes, he whispered, "I'm all in, Eve. Wherever this road takes us, I want to be right there by your side. Taking the same risks, following the same hopes." He picked up his Santa beard. "I'll have my parents call and schedule a time on Christmas day to bring Katie over to pick up Bella."

Eve's eyes widened. "Your parents? But I thought you…"

"I think I need to give you a little space for a while, don't you?" His smile didn't reach his eyes. "I'm still your friend, Eve. Always will be, no matter what. I'm only a phone call away if you need me for anything." He stared long and hard at her. "I've crossed over that friend line. I'm ready to see where this relationship can go. Until you're on the same page, I think the best thing will be a little distancing for a while. You need time to think. I need time to remember the boundaries of friendship." He grinned, gave her a mock salute and moved toward the door.

Eve's emotions tumbled in a confused mess. She didn't know what to say so she said nothing.

He turned in the doorway and studied her for several heartbeats. When he spoke his voice had a sad lilt. "I know this Christmas is going to be difficult for you. I'm sorry, Eve. I really am. I wish there was something I could do to make it easier. But I've learned the hard way that everyone grieves in their own way and in their own time. I'll wait, Eve. The possibility of us is worth waiting for." His tone took on a determined note. "But, please, for both our sakes, don't take that step until you are truly ready." His eyes locked with hers, his voice quiet and sad. "I can't...and won't...try to compete with a ghost."

Eve made no attempt to wipe away the tears running freely down her face as she watched the door close behind him.

Eve lit the fireplace and turned on the Christmas tree lights. Opting for easy listening music instead of Christmas music tonight, she turned the volume low allowing it to provide a relaxed and pleasurable background aura in the room. She poured herself a glass of wine and pulled her grandmother's afghan over her legs. Bella curled into a ball beside her on the sofa.

And, surprises never ceasing, Pug curled on the floor by her feet.

Unsure whether it was the Christmas season or the addition of Bella to his world, Pug seemed like a changed, happier, more docile dog. He still followed Eve everywhere she went but, instead of hovering in the doorways, he actually stayed under foot. The biggest change came at night. He'd started coming upstairs and sleeping at the foot of her bed. He no longer kept nightly vigils by the front door for Bryan—and that thought both gladdened and saddened her.

Eve took a sip of wine. She was happy for Pug. The poor dog had missed Bryan so much this past year. Watching him chase Bella around the house, or play with his favorite chew toy, or not even try to steal anyone's food anymore gave her hope that he not only accepted Bryan wasn't coming back but seemed to be able to find happiness again. She just hoped when the McGruders took Bella home with them tomorrow that he wouldn't revert back to his old self.

And what about me? When am I going to be able to say good-bye, move forward and reach out for a little bit of happy?

A chill slid down her spine and she tucked the afghan around her a bit tighter. Loneliness and grief are cold companions.

Her gaze roamed over ever branch of the tree, touched on every ornament, allowed her memories of past Christmases to wash over her. Surprisingly, the memories brought a smile to her lips instead of tears to her eyes. She missed Bryan. She knew, in some ways, she always would. They had shared so many wonderful Christmases together. She couldn't be sad when the memories came flooding in.

She saw the ornament they'd purchased on their trip to Manhattan, skirted the tiny slot machine they brought back from Vegas, and a smile tugged at her lips as she stared at the miniature replica of Niagara Falls. Her imagination could almost feel the spray of the water on her face. She kept perusing the tree, finding several more ornaments that fell into her favorite category. Oh, yes, definitely the small house which was as close a replica to their first home together that they'd been able to find. She smiled at the ballerina with a cloth tutu and real feathers they'd gotten in a craft fair in St. Augustine. She laughed at the Snoopy ornament Bryan had insisted upon. She chuckled at the small pug dog wearing the Santa hat as she remembered how Pug had looked this year clad in his reindeer ears for the Women's Guild Children's Party.

There it was—a past memory living happily side-by-side with a new memory. *Thanks, Pug.*

And then her eyes found it.

The brightly lit gazebo with miniature skaters.

Michael...

She couldn't believe how much she missed him these past six days. But she did. She missed his crooked grin. The sound of his laughter. His laid back attitude about everything. His sense of humor. His brilliant blue eyes. The way he cocked his head to the side and listened, really listened, when they talked.

She missed *him.*

His musky male scent tumbled together with the fresh scent of the outdoors and evergreens. The softness of his touch despite his weather-beaten hands. The way the skin crinkled beside his eyes when he smiled. The way those eyes showed her so many things—his attraction, his compassion, his empathy, his passion, his fear. And his kisses...

There weren't enough words to describe how it felt to share one breath...with him.

She stared at the ornament and could almost feel his arm slide around her waist, his body press against hers as they slid across the ice, the wind tossing her hair, the cold coloring her cheeks.

She took another sip of wine and then held the glass up and offered a salute. "Thank you, Michael. For understanding. For being my friend. Teaching me to skate. Sharing your family with me. Helping to choose and decorate this humongous tree. The tree is beautiful."

And it was.

She stared at the tree long into the night, her mind barraged with memories and her heart torn—between the past and the present, between the man she'd loved since childhood and the man whom she believed she could love.

When does grief end? When is it time to say a final good-bye?

Lost in thought, Eve silently watched the flickering of the firelight.

Sixteen

"Hi, Mom. Yes, I can see everybody," Eve said as her mother moved over and let Connie and her husband fill the screen. "Hi, Connie. Merry Christmas, Robert. Good to see you." She laughed as her nieces, Angela and Brittany, pushed their parents out of the FaceTime frame. "Us, too. Don't forget us," they chorused, leaning forward and making silly smiley faces at Eve.

Eve chuckled and tucked her robe around her as she settled onto the sofa in the den. "How could Aunt Eve forget the two of you? Never happen."

Connie pushed her computer screen back on her end giving them a wider screen shot and allowing Eve the opportunity to see everyone perched around their Christmas tree. "Your tree is awesome," Connie said. "It's huge! How did you manage getting it into the house and set it up all on your own?"

Eve glanced over her shoulder, again admiring the lit tree, and then back to her computer screen. "It is beautiful, isn't it? I had help. Michael, one of the owners of McGruder's Tree Farm delivered the tree, set it up, and even helped me decorate it."

"The tree farm guy helped decorated, too? I didn't know that was one of the services they offered," Connie teased. Her sister's lips twisted in a lame attempt to hide her smile. "Now that I think about it, Mom did mention something to me about you having a new friend."

Eve rolled her eyes. "I'm sure she did."

Both sisters laughed.

"So is he coming by today?" Connie asked. "Do you have any Christmas plans?"

That happy feeling slid right out of Eve's body but she tried not to let it show.

"Nah," she said. "His parents are dropping by later this morning to pick up, Bella, the dog I've been taking care of for him, but that's about it. Should be a quiet Christmas." She forced the widest grin she could onto her face. "And that's fine with me. I've been much busier than expected this month. I am looking forward to curling up later in front of a blazing fire with a good book and a glass of wine."

"Mom, can we open our presents now?" Her nieces could barely contain their enthusiasm as they raced around her chair and pulled on the arms of her robe.

Brittany, the youngest one, hopped up and down at her side. "Can I open my presents? I can hardly wait another minute. Please, Mommy." The five-year-old reached up and pushed Connie's chin in the direction of the Christmas tree. "Santa came, Mommy. See."

The adults laughed and the girls were given permission to start opening their presents while dad supervised.

"Ohhhh," Connie groaned, leaning closer to the monitor and stage whispering to Eve. "A roaring fire, a glass of wine, and a little bit of quiet and solitude. I hope Santa has gift-wrapped something like that under my tree this year."

Connie positioned her laptop at a better angle so Eve could see everyone. The excitement and frenzy of Christmas morning in Florida began. Eve's mother opened the soft plush robe and matching slippers Eve sent her. Her mom stroked the material and immediately slid on the slippers quickly. She also seemed to truly appreciate receiving the newest book from one of her favorite authors. But it was the surprised and pleased look on her face when she opened the cameo broach that helped Eve replace her fake grin with a genuine smile.

"Oh, honey, it's lovely," her mother said. "Thank you."

"You're welcome. I found it in a little shop on Main Street and couldn't resist."

Connie loved the paint supplies and did an absolute squeal over the one day spa treatment certificate she'd sent. "Thanks, Eve. You have no idea how much I'm going to look forward to using this," Connie said, as she waved the certificate in the air.

Eve glanced over her shoulder at the girls ripping the wrappings off their gifts and screaming in delight and she chuckled, "I think I have an idea."

The rest of the telephone call was one of shared and happy chaos. Robert appreciated the season pass tickets she'd sent him for the upcoming spring baseball season. The girls, spoiled by all including herself, flitted from one gift to another not seeming to know which present to concentrate on or play with first.

Connie obligingly opened the gifts her family sent her, as well, and did her best to show honest appreciation and holiday spirit although shadowy ghosts of both past and present pulled at her heart.

Two men. Both missing. Both missed. *How did she ever get herself into this mess?*

The phone call lasted a full hour and, surprisingly, Eve was sorry to say good-bye. She loved her family. She missed them and promised herself that next year they would all be together for the holiday. All of them needed to put their arms around each other and help each other heal. She hadn't been the only one who had lost Bryan—and his zany antics and pranks, particularly at this time of year, were missed by all.

Before she hung up, the faces of both Connie and her mom filled her entire screen and she could see from the look in their eyes and the expressions on their faces that they were missing her, too.

"I'm not going to call you, tomorrow, Eve." Her mother's voice sobered. "Not because I don't want to or because I won't be thinking about you but…well, I think the day will pass easier if you spend it by yourself. You know for reflection and enjoying memories and resting and…" Her mom's eyes filled with tears.

Eve actually reached out and touched the screen. "Don't, mom. Everything's okay. I'll be okay tomorrow, too. I promise."

Her mother sniffed and nodded. "I know, honey." Then she moved out of screen shot.

Connie watched her mother move away, then turned back to face Eve. "Don't worry. The kids will have her playing dolls and dress up in no time." Connie sobered and stared at her for an extra minute before saying, "We love you, you know. I wish you had come here for Christmas with Mom." She touched the screen with her fingers. "But I understand why you didn't. We miss him, too."

Eve returned the smile. "I know." Her eyes burned with tears she was determined not to let fall. "Now, go. Be with your family. I promise, next year we will all be together for the holiday."

Connie choked up and nodded. "Merry Christmas, little sister."

"Back at you." Eve blew a kiss and ended the call.

Eve smoothed her dark blue sweater with an outdoor snowy landscape scene over her black dress slacks and slid her feet into matching black flats. She took a little extra time today applying a touch of light gold to her eyelids, applying mascara to her lashes, and finishing with a bright red lipstick before standing back and examining herself in the mirror. It had been a long time—too long—since she wore make-up or was overly concerned about her appearance, and it felt good to dress up and put make-up on, again. She felt good.

She debated what to do with her hair. She reached up and held it up with the ends flopping on the top of her head, tried pulling it back in a bun, thought about a ponytail and then decided Christmas needed something simple and natural and pretty so she let her long auburn locks fall in waves across her shoulders and down her back.

One more spin in front of the floor length mirror on the back of her bedroom closet door and she grinned.

Perfect.

Too bad no one would be around to notice.

Hey, it's Christmas. She chastised herself immediately. *I'm doing this for myself. I notice how good I look and this year that's enough.* She chuckled. *Maybe Pug will notice. He hasn't seen me in make-up for a very long time.*

Speaking of Pug…

The little porky dog was dutifully sitting at her feet and watching her every move. He must have been able to read her mind, though, because, when she looked at him, Pug tried to make a getaway dash but she was faster. She scooped him up, carried him to the bed, and dressed him in his Santa Claus outfit, including hat and fake beard.

She snapped a picture of him on her cell phone. "You look fabulous, Pug, simply fabulous." Laughing, she lowered him from the bed to the floor. She watched for a minute to see if he'd paw at the beard, trying to get it off. Surprisingly, he didn't. He actually strutted and swayed his back end past Bella as if he was showing off and Eve laughed harder.

Bella's turn.

Eve had given the dog a bath the night before so she'd be clean and smell good for Katie. Now she gave a final combing to Bella's fur. She tied a big red bow around the dog's neck. Then clutching the dog in her arms, she gave her a big hug, and then scooted the dog into her travel kennel. "I'm going to miss you, Bella," she said through the wire door. "Pug's going to miss you, too. But I know you're going to be so happy in your new home. You're going to fall in love with Katie."

Pug roamed back and forth in front of the kennel and shot occasional looks Eve's way. Poor dog couldn't understand why Bella wasn't being allowed out to play. Heaven help everyone when Bella left for good, today.

Poor Pug.

Poor me. I know how he's going to feel. It's been six days since I've seen or spoken to Michael. If it's been this hard for a mere week, what is the rest of my life going to look like?

She couldn't rid herself of her surprise at how unexpected and how quickly this man had slid into her life—and, admittedly, into her heart. But knowing what a great guy Michael is, her growing feelings for him shouldn't surprise her, at all. The question wasn't why she cared for him but what she planned on doing about it.

Eve picked up Bella's travel kennel and deposited it in the alcove by the kitchen pantry so Katie wouldn't see it when she first arrived. Pug trotted in on her heels, plopped down beside Bella's kennel, and whined.

"I know, Pug. Believe me, I understand. But Bella belongs to Katie. Maybe I can take you over for a visit now and then." Eve poured some hot water into a mug, grabbed her Cinnamon Apple tea bag, and sat at the kitchen table. She steeped the bag several times enjoying the scent while she watched Bella scrunch her nose against the kennel gate and Pug scrunch his already pushed-in nose against hers.

Ahhh, true love.

Eve sipped her tea. She'd spent the past year missing a very special man every day of that year. Instead of allowing time to fade that longing and try to make herself feel better, what had she done? She'd added a second, really nice guy to the lets-sit-here-and-mope list. She was spending Christmas Day missing *two* men.

Eve stared at the wedding ring set on her left hand. Why isn't there a checklist or book, like a farmer's almanac or something to get people through their grief? She needed a book stating this is how many days you cry. This is the day you pack up his clothes and give them to charity. This is the day you laugh for the first time. Sure, you'll feel a twinge of guilt because you found a little piece of happiness but that's normal and it will get better over time. This is the day you'll go through an entire day and not think about him, at all. Guilt grows. Yep. But so does happiness. With any luck, during the battle between guilt and happy, happy wins.

Yep, she wishes there was a book specifically outlining each step of the process. She always liked checklists.

And then there was dating.

She sighed heavily before taking another sip of her tea and continuing with her musings.

What is the date you begin dating? Is it based on how long you were married? Or how long your spouse was sick? Is it based on what society thinks is acceptable? If so, what is acceptable? A month? Six months? A year? Ever?

When you do decide to look at someone else…date someone else…love someone else—how long do you carry the weight of that guilt?

Eve twisted her wedding ring back and forth on her finger. Slowly she slid it up a smidgeon. Before she knew it she had it past her first knuckle and then well on its way past her second knuckle. Almost off. Almost. Could she do it? Could she take it off? Could she purposely sever that one last visible tie to Bryan?

The doorbell rang.

Eve startled, slid the ring back on and followed a barking Pug who beat her to the front door. "Move, Pug." She shooed the dog back. "I need room to let them in."

When she opened the front door, Katie burst forward and wrapped her little arms around Eve. "Merry Christmas, Miss Eve."

"Merry Christmas, Katie." Eve glanced at Ruth and Tom McGruder standing behind their granddaughter, wished them a happy holiday and then offered her undivided attention to the girl. "Did you have a nice Christmas morning?"

Katie hopped and twirled in the foyer. "Look, Pug's dressed up just like Santa Claus."

Eve laughed while she held the door wide and beckoned the McGruders to come inside.

By now, Katie was on the floor and laughing as Pug licked any possible remnants of breakfast from her face. Still giggling and petting the dog, she looked up and answered Eve's question. "I got a gazillion presents. I got presents from Grandma and Grandpa and Uncle Danny and Daddy." The girl jumped to her feet. "Santa Claus left me a note on his empty cookie plate."

"He did?"

"Uh-huh. He said he left a really special present for me at your house. Did he bring a present here for me?"

The hopeful expression on Katie's face made Eve chuckle. "He certainly did. I took a peek and I think you are going to love it."

Katie clapped her hands together and did a little hop. "Can I see the present?"

Eve laughed. "Let everybody hang up their coats. Then, we'll go see what Santa left here for you." The McGruders removed their coats and hung them in the hall closet. Eve started to close the front door. The sight of the man standing on the stoop, his arms laden with brightly wrapped packages, froze her in place.

Michael.

Seventeen

"Merry Christmas, Eve," Michael smiled. "May I come in?"

She recovered from her shock and stepped back. "Of course, come in." She held the door open wide and then closed it behind him.

Michael handed the gifts to his parents. He shrugged out of his coat and hung it up.

"I didn't expect to see you, today," Eve whispered in his ear. She breathed in a male cologne she hadn't smelled on him before, a delicious male scent, and she found herself tempted to move closer for a better whiff.

"I wasn't going to, at first," he grinned broadly and whispered back. "I wanted to see the expression on my daughter's face when she meets Bella."

"I'm glad you changed your mind." Eve turned her attention to the others and gestured, "Everybody go down to the end of the hall and make a right into the den. Make yourself at home. I set up some finger-food refreshments on the table by the fireplace."

Katie and Pug raced toward the den with Sean and Ruth in close pursuit.

When Eve started to follow, Michael gently grasped her elbow and held her in place. When the others were out of sight, Michael turned her to face him. "Seeing Katie meet Bella isn't my only reason for being here."

"It's not?" Her heart fluttered in her chest. *It was so good to see him.* At this moment, she didn't care why he came, only that he had.

He smiled. "I had to see you. It's Christmas."

The nearness of his body and the touch of his hands on her arms sent heat rushing through her veins.

He is so damn masculine…handsome…sexy. Lord, help me.

His expression sobered. "I couldn't have stayed away even if I'd wanted to." He gathered her closer and locked his gaze with hers. "I missed you."

Three simple words and they meant—everything.

"I missed you, too," she whispered.

"No pressure, Eve. No expectations. Promise." He reached up and smoothed his palm down her hair and across her shoulder. "I'm here as a friend. And I'll stay a friend as long as you need me to be."

Friend? Oh Michael, friend is the last word I think of when I'm with you.

He smiled into her eyes. "C'mon. Let's join the others. My parents won't be able to keep Katie patient much longer."

"Bella's in her travel kennel in the kitchen. I'll go get her."

Michael stopped her. "No. You go in and be with the family. I'll get her." He grinned. "I remember where the kitchen is." Without another word he was gone.

Katie was standing by the Christmas tree when Eve entered the den. She had her little hands fisted on her hips and a puzzled expression on her face. "I don't see any presents under the tree, Miss Eve. No presents anywhere. Are you sure Santa came to your house?" Before Eve could answer, Katie said, "That's okay, Miss Eve. We brought you presents for Christmas. Want to see?"

What a precious little girl. She's concerned that I don't have anything to open.

Katie raced over to her grandparents, who were seated on the sofa, and lifted one of the smaller gifts. "See. This one has your name on it. I helped Grandma wrap it. Can I help you open it, too?"

"Let's wait for your father before anyone opens any gifts," Eve said. "He'll be here in just a minute." Eve sat cross-legged on the floor by the tree, then gestured for Katie to join her. No sooner were they seated than Pug decided this had to be a game designed just for him. The dog jumped from one lap to another. Katie's giggles were infectious and brought smiles and chuckles to everyone.

"What am I missing?" Michael's voice carried from the doorway. All eyes turned his way, and he said, "Katie, look what Santa Claus left for you. I found it in the kitchen."

Katie looked up and Eve wasn't prepared for the child's reaction. She'd expected squeals, laughter, running, exuberance. Instead, the child sat in silence, her eyes wide, her mouth open, and stared as her father entered the room and moved toward them. When Eve looked at the girl again, she saw a tear rolling down her cheek.

"Is it a dog?" Katie whispered, almost as if she was afraid it might be some unkind joke.

Michael laughed and set the kennel down. "I was wondering the same thing myself when I saw this little bundle of joy. But Miss Eve assures me that it is definitely a dog. Her name is Bella." He opened the kennel door. Bella darted out and straight into Katie's arms.

Then it started—total and awesome bedlam. Bella and Pug filled Katie's arms and lavished wet doggie kisses anywhere and everywhere they could. The sound of pure joy wafted through the air on Katie's giggles.

"Hi, Bella. I'm Katie." She hugged the dog, let her go, and then hugged her again. She looked up, tears gone, and said, "Isn't she beautiful, Daddy? Bella is the best present I ever got. Do I get to keep her? Please, Daddy. Can I keep Bella?"

Michael squatted down, removed the big red bow from Bella, and actually reached out to pet her. "Sure, you can keep her, honey. She's your present. But you have to promise to take very good care of her. You have to feed her and walk her and play with her every day. Can you do that?"

"Yes, Daddy. I can. I promise." She picked Bella up, the dog hanging almost the entire length of Katie's height, and carried the dog over to the sofa to show her grandparents.

"See?" Eve gave Michael a playful poke in the ribs. "I told you Katie would think Bella was beautiful."

"Yes, you did." Michael grinned and shook his head. "What is that old adage? Beauty is in the eye of the beholder."

At that moment, Sean came over and whispered to the two of them. "Didn't they have any good-looking animals in that shelter? This has to be one of the ugliest critters I've ever seen. I wasn't even sure it was a dog when it first came out of that kennel of yours."

Michael and Eve burst out laughing.

Eve opened the gifts from the McGruders. Sean gave her a gift certificate for a fresh evergreen tree for next Christmas. Ruth gave her a laminated recipe book filled with her own recipes, including the secret ingredient she puts in her apple pies.

Awkwardly, Eve handed them a gift-wrapped tray of homemade Christmas cookies. "I'm so sorry. I didn't think we'd be exchanging gifts. All I have for you are cookies."

Ruth accepted the tray, moved the ribbon so she could peer through the clear wrapping, and smiled. "These look absolutely delicious, my dear. My family will tell you, I love to bake cakes and pies, but I don't usually find the time to do cookies. This tray will probably disappear within an hour of making it home. You couldn't have given us a better gift."

The adults settled back and were totally amused at the antics of Katie, Bella, and Pug. As the afternoon progressed, everyone sang Christmas carols, nibbled on cookies, ate the rest of the finger foods, and, as always seemed to happen when they got together as a group, took part in a variety of conversations and debates.

This isn't how she'd envisioned Christmas this year. She'd expected to be alone. She had wanted to be alone or she would have gone with her mother to Florida.

But something had changed.

She had changed…was continuing to change. She was beginning to realize there would always be a part of her heart that would grieve for Bryan—but this family was showing her a life beyond grief, a journey they'd taken themselves. They showed her how to move forward, a step at a time, sometimes an inch at a time, but move forward they did. They spoke, freely and fondly, of Michael's wife, Susan, making sure Katie was raised with wonderful stories to cherish about her mother. They gave Eve a glimpse of what a tomorrow after grief could look like.

Michael sat cross-legged on the floor playing with Katie, Bella, and Pug. He chose that particular second to look up and their eyes locked. He smiled, winked, and returned his attention to his daughter. A simple gesture but one that made her smile in return, warmed her heart, fueled her hope.

Sean announced it was time to call it a day and head home. Ruth agreed and began gathering Bella's chew toys, extra cans of dog food, leash and travel carrier. Katie made a big fuss over saying good-bye to

Pug and invited the dog to come and visit, anytime.

Eve accompanied the group to the front door. She'd had a wonderful afternoon and was genuinely sorry to see it end. The elder McGruders helped Katie carry Bella's travel kennel to the car. Michael lingered in the foyer. He reached into his coat pocket and pulled out a small, square, brightly wrapped Christmas present.

"Merry Christmas, Eve." He placed the thin box in her hand. "This is for you."

Eve looked down at the silvery paper and red bow. Her stomach dropped. "Oh Michael, I didn't get anything for you."

"Open it," he said. "This gift is from Santa Claus for both of us." Michael grinned. "And be sure to read the note inside before you say anything."

Butterflies danced in her stomach as she removed the ribbon, peeled away the wrapping, and slowly removed the lid. She lifted the note from the top of the tissue paper.

Michael McGruder would like to invite his friend, Eve Carlson, to welcome in the New Year with him. Dinner, music, and an overall good time will be provided.

Eve pushed aside the tissue paper. Inside were two tickets to one of the hottest venues in town, and it didn't hurt that the restaurant rested on top of a hill and had a reputation of having one of the most spectacular views in the state.

"Michael…"

He clasped her hand and spoke before she could. "Just two friends, Eve, welcoming the beginning of a new year, together. I promise. Just a night of good food, good music, a little bit of rusty dancing maybe on my part, and good conversation. Please say yes."

Her stomach somersaulted and her pulse raced. *Friends only?* Did she want to accept this invitation as merely friends when every fiber of her body tried to pull her mind and her heart into a much deeper relationship?

With wisdom comes clarity and Eve knew exactly what she wanted. She slid her fingertips down the smoothness of Michael's cheek and smiled into his eyes. "Thank you, Michael. Be sure to thank Santa for me, too. This is a lovely Christmas gift. I'll look forward to it."

Michael's face burst into a grin. "Fantastic. I'll pick you up at seven.

Now I'm going to get out of here. I don't want to give you the chance to change your mind. Plus neither one of us wants Dad to get impatient and start blowing the horn." He leaned forward and brushed her lips with a quick, gentle kiss. "Merry Christmas, Eve."

In a flash, he turned and bolted down the sidewalk.

Eve fastened Pug's leash and took him with her onto the front stoop. She waved as the McGruder's car backed down the drive, and continued to wave until the tail lights disappeared.

A calmness washed over her. A dash of hope.

Eve took Pug for his nightly walk down the block, her mind replaying the day's events and conversations. She could no longer deny that Michael and his family were already nestled in the folds of her heart. The sheer delight on Michael's face and the happiness in his eyes when she'd accepted his invitation made her happy. Imagine how much happier he was going to feel when he realized that, if she had her way, New Year's would be ushered in as much more than mere friends.

Due to the severity of Bryan's illness, they hadn't been physically intimate for several years. She missed Bryan, of course. But she also missed the intimacy of lying in a man's arms, of giving and taking, of being a woman enjoying a physical relationship with a man.

She found herself wanting to take that next, natural step…with Michael. Every time she saw him it got harder to keep her hands off his hard, toned body. She wanted to lightly trail her fingertips across his naked skin. She wanted to feel his hands…and his mouth…explore her body as she longed to explore his. She had to admit to herself, though, that a jitter of nerves and light apprehension raced up and down her spine. She'd only been with one man in her entire life. Would she be enough for Michael?

The man's face appeared in her mind's eye, his kind and laughing eyes, his smile, his patience.

She smiled and she knew, without the shadow of a doubt. She might have an awkward moment, here and there, but she was willing to try. Michael might have gotten to the "I'm-all-in" part of their relationship a bit faster than she did, but she'd arrived. She, too, was all in. She was ready to take a chance on the future and see where this relationship could go.

Or, at least, she would be by New Year's Eve.

She still had one more thing she had to do, one more final good-bye she had to say.

Eighteen

Eve carried her morning coffee mug with her into the den and placed it on the end table. She pulled her wedding picture off the mantle and carried it to the sofa where she wrapped herself in their Christmas afghan. She gazed at the young couple staring back at her, so happy, so in love, so oblivious to what the future had in store.

"We were happy, weren't we, Bryan?" She lovingly traced his face. "We were just kids back then. We looked at the world with such optimism. We truly believed we could handle anything as long as we faced it together." She sighed. "We knew one day that one of us would have to bury the other." She frowned. "When we were old and decrepit, remember? We swore we'd die together in our sleep at the ripe old age of one hundred."

Her smile was bittersweet.

Well, part of that came true, didn't it, love?

Her mind immediately took her back to their last night together. How she'd climbed onto the hospital bed with him, draped her arm over him. They'd listened to Christmas music, talked about everything and nothing, stared at the lights on the tree. She'd kissed him, not realizing it was their last kiss, and fell asleep with her head on his chest. They'd been happy, even then.

"I can't believe it's been a year, Bryan. In some ways it feels like a hundred years since I've been able to see you, or talk to you, or touch you and in other ways it seems like yesterday," she said into empty air. "I remember that final night with such clarity. I can almost see your smile when I walked into the room. I can almost feel your body curled against mine as I laid down beside you. I can almost hear your heart beating beneath my ear when I placed my head on your chest. Almost."

She looked away from the picture and glanced around the empty room. "I can't see you now but I know you're still here, aren't you? Still watching over me. Still loving me." She blinked back threatening tears. "I miss you so much, Bryan Carlson. So, so much."

Pug caught her attention with a whine. She reached down and pulled the dog onto the sofa with her. "I know you still miss him, too, don't you, Pug, even if you don't do night watch by the door anymore? Now, you're going to be missing Bella, too. And I can't explain it to you. Poor Pug. No one prepared you for it to be just the two of us, again, did they?" She gently rubbed the top of the dog's head. "It's going to be all right, buddy. We're going to be all right. I promise."

Pug circled and settled down against her hip.

Eve gazed at the lights on the Christmas tree and listened to the faint music in the background. She allowed her memories to carry her back to last Christmas. Family visitors had come and gone, wishing Bryan a Merry Christmas when everyone knew it was truly their good-bye visit. Eve had dismissed the evening hospice nurse once Bryan had been made comfortable for the evening, so the nurse could spend the rest of the evening with her own family.

"If we could choose a perfect evening, that was it, wasn't it, Bryan?" Eve said. "You were alert. You weren't in pain. For those few hours, you didn't feel weak or sick. For that brief period of time, you were simply Bryan, the man I loved."

She remembered how reluctant the hospice nurse had been to leave early. She'd taken Eve aside and told her that, in her experience, sometimes people rally right before they pass. They're as pain free as possible and many have come to terms with their situation. It's almost like a tiny gift of time to say a final good-bye. She stressed it doesn't happen all the time, but wanted her to be prepared just in case. She asked again if Eve was sure she wanted her to go.

"You know me, Bryan. Did I listen? Heck, no. I sent her home. Truthfully, I have never regretted it. The nurse got that little bit of time with the people she loved. I got privacy and precious time, for the first time in too long, with the one I loved."

Eve shook her head. She didn't know why she'd brushed off the nurse's words. Maybe because she thought it was something to expect down the road, or maybe she just couldn't face the fact, yet, that death was going to happen, at all.

But that night…

That night would stay in her memory and in her heart for the rest of her life.

Eve set the picture on the end table and picked up her coffee mug. She smiled at her husband's image. "So, Bryan, you and I need to have a talk." She took another swig of coffee. *Maybe I should lace it with brandy for liquid courage,* she thought. Then, she chuckled. When had she ever been afraid to have a conversation with Bryan?

It's time.

Eve sighed, then began to speak to the man she couldn't see but never doubted was still there.

"I met a man, Bryan. His name is Michael. He's a widower with a four-year-old little girl. Here name is Katie and she'll be five in a couple of weeks. She's absolutely adorable. You'd love her." She reached over and petted Pug. "Pug introduced us. You probably know that already, don't you? Knowing you and how you loved pranks, I bet it was you who told Pug to jump out the truck window in the first place."

She smiled. "Michael is one of the good guys, Bryan. He's smart, kind, hard-working, loyal, family-oriented, has a great sense of humor. If you met him, I know you would like him. And we've become friends…good friends…close friends…more than friends…" Her voice trailed off.

She twisted her wedding ring.

"He's been good to me, Bryan. Patient. Kind."

She twisted the ring again.

"He thinks we might have a future together. Crazy, huh?" She paused for the longest moment. "And I do, too."

She released the breath she'd been holding. "I think I'm falling in love with him. I think he might be falling in love with me, too."

Finally, slowly, she slipped her wedding ring off her finger. "Don't be mad at me, Bryan. It's all your fault, you know. It's because I've loved you. It's because I know how beautiful a marriage with the right man can be, that's what makes me want to try to find that kind of happy again." She kissed her fingertips and then transferred the kiss to Bryan's image. "I will cherish our years together for the rest of my life."

Eve stood and, when she did, Pug jumped to the floor. Eve left a few of the smaller pictures of the two of them together sitting out but she carried her wedding picture into the bedroom. She wrapped the picture in tissue paper, lovingly placing it in the bottom of her hope chest below her beloved grandmother's afghan.

Christmas was over.

Then, Eve walked into the master bedroom closet, Pug close on her heels.

"Pug, shoo. You've gone from one extreme to the other. First you don't come near me and then you're constantly underfoot. If you're not careful, I'm going to step on your paw or something by accident but it will still hurt. So, shoo. Get out of the closet. Scoot."

Pug scooted away from her swinging arm. He settled down in the doorway, seemingly happy with doorways, again. At least, she knew he wouldn't be getting into any mischief.

Eve squatted down and worked the combination to the small safe. This particular safe kept their most important possessions—a copy of their marriage certificate, Bryan's death certificate, the diamond bracelet Bryan had given her on their fifth wedding anniversary, her grandmother's cameo broach that her mom passed down to Eve at her wedding. She reached in to slide out the velvet jewelry tray so she could place her wedding ring set inside. When she pulled out the tray, an envelope fell out onto the floor.

Eve knew immediately what it was. Another letter from Bryan. She stared at the envelope and chewed on her lower lip. She hadn't been expecting another letter, and definitely hadn't been expecting one to be hidden where only their very important items would be found.

She picked up the letter and straightened. Her fingers trembled as she opened the flap, removed the letter, and began to read.

My Sweet Evie,

I hope you found my first letter before discovering this one. Letter number one was meant for us to reminisce together about the past. Sharing our memories. Remembering good times, together.

Hopefully, you found my second letter when you pulled out the ornaments to decorate for Christmas. Christmas present, get it? You know me, always teasing, joking, and playing with you. I hope you listened to my requests, and made this Christmas festive and fun.

And, now, my dearest Evie, if you are opening the safe, then I'm assuming you've removed your wedding rings and are placing them inside.

I've got to admit this letter was the hardest one for me to write. Mainly, because I knew it would be the last surprise I could ever give you—and I'm man enough to admit it really tore up my heart.

Eve's breath caught in her throat and tears burned her eyes. She couldn't do this. She couldn't read this letter. It hurt too much to know he had thought about her removing her wedding rings long before he left this earth.

But that was Bryan.

That was exactly something Bryan would do. Write her letters.

Christmas past. Christmas present. And now, Christmas future?

So typically, Bryan. She took several deep breaths, then continued reading.

We both know it's time, Evie—knowing you, it's long past time—for you to step into your future. There's a whole world out there filled with hopes and dreams. Find them, and live each and every one. No one deserves it more.

I want you to embrace this new season of your life. I want you to be bold and confident and happy, as I know you always were and need to be again. I want you to find someone special, someone worthy of your love, to share life's adventures with you.

It's okay, Evie, to love somebody else, completely, with abandon and devotion—and to be loved with the same devotion and passion right back. That's what I want for you.

He'll be one lucky guy. I know. I could have never found a better friend, more passionate lover, or more devoted wife than you. I count my blessings for every second you were in my life.

This is my final letter, Evie. My final good-bye. Our final good-

bye.

Before I go, I want you to know, from the bottom of my heart, you were, and always will be, the love of my life. But, my sweet Evie, I was only your first love. You still have so much more love to give...so give it, and be happy.

Life goes on whether we want it to or not. So live yours. Find your next love. Buy that house with the white picket fence. Fill it with children, and laughter, and a bunch of Pugs. Lol.

Whenever you remember us, as I know you will now and then, remember us as we were. Happy.

Good-bye, my love.

Bryan

Eve clutched the letter to her chest and slid down the back wall of the closet until she was sitting on the floor. Tears became sobs as all the pain and loss over the past four years racked her body.

Whining and crying, Pug raced into the closet and jumped into her lap, whining and showering her with dog kisses.

Clutching the letter against her chest and cradling Pug in her arms, Eve sat on the floor of the closet, saying good-bye to someone they'd loved and preparing to move into the future.

Nineteen

"Happy New Year to you, too, Mom." Eve hit speaker on the phone, tossed it on the night stand, and continued to lay her clothes for the evening out on the bed. "Michael's going to pick me up around seven." She stood in front of the floor length mirror and looked at her newly purchased satin underpants from every angle. She'd never had the nerve to go without a bra but her slinky, satin gown demanded it. She wondered if she'd be showing off the tiny piece of fabric tonight, and if Michael would be pleased with what he saw if she did.

"What? Sorry, Mom. I was thinking about something else. Huh? My dress? Yes, I bought a new dress. Yes, Mom. A new dress. New shoes. The works."

New underwear, she thought with a grin.

"You're right. That's exactly what I'm doing, building new friendships and new memories for the New Year." She listened to her mom for a few more minutes before interrupting. "Mom, I have to go or I won't be ready on time. Yes, I'll send you a picture. Yes, Mom, of the dress and of Michael." Eve laughed. "Mom, stop! I know you're trying to help but you're treating me like I'm still in high school and getting ready for the prom. Relax. I'm a grown woman and I've got this handled."

Eve crossed her fingers behind her back and hoped her words were true.

"Happy New Year to you, too, Mom. I love you."

She reached over and ended the call.

Mentally, she went over everything one more time.

She lightly touched the loose, sequined clip holding her hair off her shoulders. Every hair in place. Check.

She took one final glance at her face. Make-up perfect. Check.

She carefully slid the soft, body hugging sheath over her head. She must have been out of her mind to pick this dress. But she wanted to feel bold, confident, and if this dress didn't do it for her nothing would. It clung to her every curve. It flowed and shimmered with every movement. It left absolutely nothing to the imagination, cut low in the front and almost backless. The kind of dress a super star celebrity might wear to the Oscars. Sexy as hell, but classy. Check.

She slid her feet into sequined heels and grabbed a matching sequined clutch purse. Check.

Do I really look okay? Is the dress as beautiful as I think or do I look like a middle-age fool playing dress up?

Her breath caught in her throat and her stomach flip-flopped. Well, this is as good as it gets. Hope he likes it. Hope he likes me in it…and out of it.

Ruth had come by earlier to pick up Pug for the evening which was a total relief. It would be a nice New Year for Pug, too, if he could visit with Bella and Katie.

The doorbell sounded.

Eve took one last look at herself in the mirror. Satisfied with her reflection, she hurried downstairs.

Snowing.

Hard.

Visibility twenty maybe thirty feet, at best.

Figures. His luck. Michael hoped she wouldn't use the weather as a last minute excuse to cancel. He'd been looking forward to this since Christmas and he'd be super disappointed if she bailed at the last minute. But she'd sent Pug home with his mother earlier, today. That was a good sign, right?

When he pulled up in the driveway, he left the motor running so the inside of the car would be comfortably warm when he escorted Eve out. He knocked the snow off his shoes when he reached her stoop and rang the bell.

His pulse raced and he couldn't seem to keep still. *Get it together,* he warned himself. *Friends, remember. Come on too strong and you're going to blow what might be the best thing to happen to you in years. Friends. Say it again. Friends. Got it?*

The door opened and Michael, momentarily, forgot how to breathe. She was gorgeous! His eyes slid over the bright red satin gown that complimented her auburn hair and hugged her body like a glove. A slit on the left side of the skirt drew his eyes like a magnet. No way she'd expect him to ignore that delectable view of naked calf and thigh peeking out whenever she moved, right? His libido, which, of course, didn't speak the language of friends only, agreed with him one hundred per cent.

"You look gorgeous," he said.

"Thanks." Her coy smile told him she knew exactly what she was doing to him and was enjoying every minute of it. "Come inside. I'll only be a minute."

He stepped into the foyer, shutting the door behind him. The view of her departing was equally enticing. The back of the dress, or lack of a back, plunged below her waistline and stopped right in the appropriate spot at the top of the curve of her exquisitely shaped bottom. Holy cow, he was dead in the water, his libido insisting he ignore his mind and give up any pretense of thinking he could treat her platonically.

"Is it still snowing hard outside?" Her voice drifted down the hall.

At that moment, he felt like an old cartoon where the devil sat on one shoulder and an angel on the other. The angel prompted him to tell the truth and risk the chance she'd cancel the evening. The devil didn't have to prompt him, at all. He simply flashed him a mental image of the back of Eve's dress and all that delicious naked skin.

"Michael?" She'd returned and stood in front of him. Close enough for him to appreciate the gentle, rounded swells of her breasts. Close enough to notice the delightful way she licked her lower lip. Close enough to reach out and pull her closer, but, thank God, he didn't.

"Michael, are you all right?" Her brow furrowed.

"Sorry, I had something on my mind. What did you ask me? Snow? Yes, it's still snowing but I'm sure it's nothing to be concerned about. Are you ready to go? Where's your coat?"

She pulled her coat out of the closet and he held it for her while she slipped it on. The flowery scent of her perfume tickled his nose and tempted him to lean in and nuzzle her neck for a longer whiff.

Mayday, mayday, his mind screamed. *Try spelling the word friend over and over again and see if that helps. F—as in she looks fantastic. R—as in ravenous. I—as in you are an idiot if you think you're going to make it through this evening without making a fool of yourself.*

When they pulled out of the driveway, Michael was grateful for the snow. His silence as he struggled to relax his body and get his mind back in gear could be attributed to concentrating on his driving. Thankfully, the ride to the venue took little more than a half hour. A half hour of small talk. Small smiles. And waves of desire hitting him like a tsunami. He'd thought she was beautiful without make-up and clad in jeans and a t-shirt. Tonight, she took it to a whole new level and he seriously wondered if he'd be able to control his body and not embarrass either one of them. She was gorgeous.

When they arrived, the valet parked their car while Michael checked their coats. The greeter asked them to follow him. Michael placed his hand lightly on Eve's back and a surge of heat rushed through his veins at the silky softness of her naked flesh.

This is going to be a long night, he groaned to himself.

He pulled out Eve's chair, then went around to his own. He was mesmerized, simply mesmerized, by everything about her. The candle light danced across her face and illuminated the highlights in that fiery red hair. Her smile animated her face as they shared stories about Katie, work, the dogs, and the holidays. At other times, her expression took on a sultry look of a woman confident in her own skin and well aware of the effect she was having on him.

Michael did his best to enjoy each moment and leave all hopes and expectations at the door. It didn't take more than a few bites of their meal to know why this was a five-star rated restaurant and reservations needed to be made well in advance. Lucky for him, he had wonderful, understanding parents. His father had made these reservations for his own New Year's Eve celebration months ago. Michael had never expected his parents to gift the tickets to both of them for Christmas, instead. They'd agreed to care for Katie, Pug, and Bella and insisted he could put them to better use this year than they could.

Michael grinned. He loved his parents.

As the midnight hour approached, the celebrations intensified, the crowd thickened but the music softened, and Michael was able to move Eve across the dance floor to a quiet little spot close to the corner of the room. He drew her close, his arm circling her waist, their eyes locked on each other, and they danced, swaying back and forth, beneath the foliage of a tall silk tree.

Heaven.

"Are you having a good time," Michael asked, still grinning like an idiot, still trying to maintain his promise, and losing miserably.

"I'm having a wonderful time." She smiled into his eyes and, if he didn't know better, he could have sworn she purposely leaned in closer. Her lips parted slightly and he didn't need a second invitation. He kissed her.

Not gently. Not softly. Not at all like the friend he had promised her he'd be, but deeply, demandingly like a man who desired her with an almost unbridled passion. He wanted to shout with joy when she kissed him just as passionately back.

"Michael." She whispered his name against his lips, and then reached up and cupped the side of his face with her hand…her left hand…her naked ring finger left hand. Michael pulled her hand away, looked at it in disbelief, and then his eyes shot to hers.

"Your ring?" The strangled harshness of his voice revealed all of his emotions, his hopes, his fears, his dreams, it was all there for her to see if she would only look.

"It was time." A simple sentence that told him everything.

His breath caught in his throat. Every fiber of his body ached as she touched him again, trailing her fingers ever-so-slowly down his face, down his throat, her hand sliding beneath his jacket and settling on his chest, where he was certain she could feel his heart beating like a drum.

"There is something special, something beautiful, happening between us, Michael. I feel it. I know you feel it, too." She leaned her body flush against him, giving him a satisfied, seductive smile when he could no longer hide the effect she was having on him. "I'm finally ready, Michael. I'm all in."

"Are you sure, Eve?" He held his breath, almost afraid to hear her answer.

She moved back slightly so she could look into his eyes. "I'm hoping this road will be one I get to spend a lifetime traveling with you. I'm ready to see, if you are."

"Eve…" He fought to contain his emotions. He hadn't expected this. He'd hoped. He dreamed. But he thought he'd have to dig in and wait for a very long time.

"But I have to warn you," she said, a teasing glint in her eyes. "I come with a lot of baggage."

"I knew it going in." He grinned. "Anyone that drives a monster truck and owns a flying food-stealing dog has baggage," he teased. His fingers touched her face and lingered there. "News flash, honey, I have some suitcases of my own."

She chuckled and snuggled into him.

He wrapped his arms around her. He held her close, her hair tickling his nose, her scent seeping into his lungs, the feel of her flesh awakening every male fiber in his body. "I'm only going to ask you one more time. Are you sure, Eve?" He tilted her chin and gazed into her eyes. "I'm not going anywhere if you think you might need more time," he said, softly.

She locked her gaze with his. "It will never be okay that Bryan's gone. I loved him. And there's a piece of my heart that always will."

Michael nodded his understanding.

"But Bryan is my past." Eve slid back into his arms. "You, Mr. Michael McGruder, are my present." She kissed him lightly, teasingly running the tip of her tongue along his lower lip. She smiled at him and her tone held a seriousness he'd never heard in it before. "When I dare to dream, dare to look into my future, I see you, Michael." She wrapped both arms around his waist and smiled up at him. "Only you."

The sound of silverware clinking against crystal, noisemakers, bells, and the sound of people cheering filled the air in an almost deafening roar.

Michael laughed. "I think New Year's came in when we weren't looking and we missed it."

Eve smiled widely. "We were right where we were supposed to be. We didn't miss a thing."

He held her in his arms, astounded at this change of events, and optimistic and excited about their future. He was definitely in deep, body and soul deep, and no matter what happens he wouldn't want it any other way.

"Happy New Year, Eve" he smiled into her eyes.

"Happy New Year, Michael." She smiled right back.

He pressed his forehead to hers and whispered, "Is it too soon to say I think I'm falling in love with you?"

She looped a hand around his neck and leaned into him. "I think I'm falling in love with you, too."

He ran his hands along her body, pulling her closer, cradling her flush against him and never wanting to let her go. He lowered his head and kissed her. This kiss holding a promise of happily-ever-after for both of them.

"What happens now?" he asked. He knew he wore the biggest slap-happy grin on his face but he couldn't help it.

"Let's go home, Michael." She reached up and kissed him, boldly and confidently. "And we'll find out, together."

Epilogue

Five Years Later

Eve tucked her grandmother's afghan tightly around her body and gazed into the fire. She sipped her wine and listened, contentedly, to the sounds of holiday music playing softly in the room. The tree, fully decorated and totally beautiful, stood sentry in front of the picture window that was already collecting snowflakes from the storm outside.

She loved Christmas.

Always would.

So lost in her own musings, she hadn't heard him approach and startled when his lips brushed the skin on the back of her neck.

"Michael!" She laughed and then reached up to touch his hand lying on her shoulder. "Don't sneak up on me like that. You scared me."

"Ahh," he whispered, his lips again finding that sensitive spot behind her ear. "Half the fun is knowing, after all these years, I can still surprise you." He circled the sofa and sat down beside her. He pulled out the edge of one side of the afghan to join her while simultaneously sliding his other arm around her shoulders.

"So?" she asked, handing him a glass of wine she had waiting for him. "All quiet on the home front?"

"Absolutely. Piece of cake."

"Piece of cake?" She couldn't hide the surprise in her voice. "You were gone for quite a while."

He got a sheepish expression on his face. "Well, I had to improvise. Mikey needed several burps, hugs, and pacing around the room before I could get him to nod off."

"And Katie?" Eve asked.

"She was a little harder. She's too old for bedtime stories, anymore, so I had to play two games with her before she'd say good-night."

Eve chuckled. "That's what you call a piece of cake?"

"Hey, I got them both settled for the night so we could have some alone time, didn't I?"

"Yes, you did." She smoothed her fingers down his face. "Good job, Daddy."

Michael wiggled his eyebrows. "Right now I'm not Daddy."

"You're not?" A smile spread across her face. "Okay. What should I call you?"

"Honey. Sweetheart. Lover boy," he said.

"Lover boy?" Eve struggled to hold back her giggle.

He leaned forward and kissed her—softly, tenderly, temptingly. He lifted his lips and stared into her eyes. "There's more, much more, where that came from." The huskiness in his tone told her everything she needed to know.

She rested her head on his chest, but didn't speak.

Michael stroked her hair. After a few minutes, he said, "Penny for your thoughts."

She cuddled against him. "I was thinking how lucky we are. Both of us. We both had spouses in our lives that we loved, lost, and have impacted us for eternity. And yet…" She smiled up at him. "We got a second chance, Michael. To find love. To build a family together. To be happy. Sometimes that feels like more than luck to me."

"I hear you. Like maybe we have two guardian angels named Susan and Bryan having our backs and cheering us on?" Michael grinned.

"Yeah," Eve whispered. "Something like that."

Michael pulled her closer. "Have I told you today just how beautiful you are?"

Eve kissed him lightly. "Not yet." She kissed him again, a little longer, a little more passionately. "But I'm listening."

Michael cradled her in his arms and kissed her with such passion no words were needed.

Thank you, Bryan and Susan, Eve thought. *Merry Christmas.*

Diane Burke

·

I hope you enjoyed reading Christmas Love Letters for Evie as much as I enjoyed telling Michael and Eve's story. I would greatly appreciate it if you would leave me a review. Many times readers use reviews to decide if they wish to purchase the book from an author they haven't read before. Thank you so much for your support.

Keep reading for a sneak peek of my new book Forever Love

Forever, Love

Diane Burke

One

Harrison Stone caught a glimpse of himself in the hall mirror and groaned. Blue tights, red briefs, a big red letter 'S' pinned onto his shirt, long flowing red cape. For charity or not, he couldn't believe he'd allowed his grandmother to talk him into wearing this get-up—and for a fundraising auction, no less. Was he nuts?

The sound of music, laughter, and a sea of voices drifted up the staircase of Harrison's northern New Jersey estate. He dared a quick glance over the banister. No one seemed to notice he'd slipped away. He knew he wouldn't get more than a few minutes respite before he'd have to appear on the makeshift stage for the annual Halloween Bachelor Auction Fundraiser, but he'd take what he could get.

I don't know why I put myself through this every year.

He opened the library door and slipped inside.

For charity. Remember? Think about all the kids you're helping.

He glanced down at his costume with chagrin. Charity or not, he was grateful he only had to be subjected to this humiliation once a year. Hopefully his grandmother, chairperson of the event, would find a new theme for next year's bash.

"Are you hiding, too?"

Startled by the male voice coming from behind him, Harrison spun around and then grinned. "Should have known you'd beat me up here." His grandmother had unofficially adopted Greg Cooper as a young teenager who had grown up to become his best friend and his business partner.

Greg lifted a glass with what appeared to be two fingers of Harrison's prize whiskey. "Yes, I did. And I helped myself to a little liquid courage from your private stock while I was at it. Want one?" Without waiting for an answer, he poured a generous amount of whiskey into a second glass and slid it across the desktop.

Harrison lifted the glass, gestured bottoms up, and took a healthy gulp. The warm liquid slid down his throat and almost made him forget the reason the two of them were hiding out in the library in the first place. Almost. He eyed his friend who was covered with individual-sized empty cereal boxes, and grinned. "I give up. What are you supposed to be?"

A rubber knife and ski mask rested on the edge of the desk. Greg stood up, spun around and gestured with one hand at the boxes covering his shirt front and back. "Can't you tell? I'm a serial killer. Get it?"

Harrison burst out laughing.

"Don't knock it. I'm fully expecting to claim the Most Frightening prize this year, or at least Most Original."

"You don't have to wear a costume to snag that prize." Harrison perched a hip on the edge of his mahogany desk and took another swig of his drink.

"You think you're a funny guy, huh? Have you looked in the mirror lately? I'm not the one walking around in tights, red briefs, and a cape."

"Grandmother thought the costume would bring a higher bid in the auction."

Now Greg laughed. "Patrice might be an older woman, but she still knows what the ladies want. What do you think she's showing off? Your abs? Your muscled thighs? Or maybe..."

Harrison raised a hand. "Enough. Point made." A heated flush crept up his neck and burned his face. *Damn!* Charity or not, he hated being paraded around like a slab of prime beef.

Greg laughed harder. "Hey, don't sweat it, buddy. All of us hate this. Grandmother manages to wrangle all the wealthy single men within a hundred mile radius. Then she gets us to dress in ridiculous outfits, auctions us off for a night of dinner and dancing. And none of us, not one, has the nerve to tell her no. Don't know how she does it."

"She shows us pictures of sick kids all year long until we can't stand it anymore."

"True. But I am perfectly willing to write a sizable check. Why do we have to suffer through the humiliations of an auction?"

"Because she is a brilliant business woman. Grandmother gets a sizable check from all of us anyway. And then she doubles that contribution with the proceeds from the auction. Pretty savvy if you ask me." Harrison shrugged. "Besides, it's not that bad. I don't suppose we should be complaining It's only one night out of the year."

"That's easy for you to say. You seem to get all the beautiful eligible ladies starting a bidding war over you. Last year I got stuck with Gladys Jabernecky."

Harrison tried to hide his chuckle as he took another sip of his drink.

"Yeah, go ahead, laugh. You didn't have to slow dance with her. She's four inches taller than me and three hundred pounds if she's an ounce. I thought I'd smother to death squeezed against those size fifty-two boobs. And she had the nerve to put a death grip on my ass while we danced!"

Harrison choked on his drink as he remembered how hysterical the scene had been.

Greg waved his hand up and down his shirt. "This year, though, I'm prepared. No matter who wins the bid, there will be tons of cereal boxes between us."

"Smart move." Harrison raised his glass in a toast. "Chalk it up to a good cause, buddy. It's only dinner conversation and a few dances."

"Easy for you to say. Every hot babe in the room bids on you. I get stuck with the leftovers."

"Only because, Mr. Playboy, you've done the naughty dance with most of them already. Do you think it's easy for me? These ladies don't want a dance. They want dibs on being the next Mrs. Harrison Stone. I swear all I see is dollar signs in their eyes."

"Ouch! Seven years later and you still think every woman you meet is like your gold-digging ex-wife, Cynthia?"

Harrison shrugged a shoulder. "What's that old saying? Fool me once, shame on you. Fool me twice, shame on me?" He waved a dismissive hand. "Let's not spoil what's left of the evening rehashing history."

"I'm not the one stuck in the past." Greg came around the desk and placed a hand on Harrison's shoulder. "You can't keep comparing every new woman you meet to Cynthia. Big mistake, bro."

Harrison sighed. "It always ends up about money. Doesn't anyone fall in love anymore?"

Greg rolled his eyes and plopped back down in the nearest chair.

"It's *always* going to involve your money. You're loaded. Plus, you're easy on the eyes and you're single. That's a pretty hard package for any woman to pass up."

Greg wasn't wrong. Harrison's software designs combined with the two tech companies he'd sold had earned him billions—on top of his family inheritance. But wasn't he worth more to a woman than just a wallet and a handsome face?

"Is it wrong to want more?" Harrison knew he sounded maudlin, but this subject cut him to the core. "How can I build a life, start a family, if I'm never sure I'm anything more than a dollar sign to my partner?"

Greg chuckled. "Easy. Draw up a prenup. Give the new lady in your life a generous allowance for every year she's your wife, but don't hand her the key to the cash box. That's the only sane way to do things these days."

He leaned forward and pointed his index finger at Harrison. "Better yet, have her sign away all rights to your money. She wouldn't get a red cent in a divorce. If you can find a woman who will sign that little piece of paper, you'll know she loves just you—or that she's absolutely crazy—or both."

Harrison looked around the room like he was seeing it for the first time. The heavy brocade drapes, the polished wood floors, the thick burgundy, green and beige rug centered in the middle of the room, the mahogany bookcases overflowing with a mixture of bestsellers, as well as priceless collectible editions.

He turned and stared out the window, taking in the stables, the undulating meadows and woods and pond that comprised the estate. With a sudden clarity that weighed heavily on his soul, he knew Greg was right. Everything he saw, everywhere he looked, was a testament to his wealth. How could he fault the women in his life for being influenced by it?

"I'd gladly walk away from all of this if it meant I could find a woman who would love me for myself." The truth in Harrison's words weighed heavily on him.

Greg stood and poured himself another drink. He held up the bottle to offer a refill but Harrison shook his head. "Face it, Harrison. You think there's this mystical creature hiding somewhere out there who doesn't give a damn about money, who would love you even if you were as poor as a church mouse. Well, that's just nuts. All women are motivated by money. Every last one of them."

Harrison opened his mouth to speak, but Greg raised his palm to stop him.

"Hey, I don't blame them, and you shouldn't either,' Greg said. "Think about it. You were born into wealth. You wouldn't know how to exist without money. You've had servants jumping at your beck and call since you took your first breath." Greg drew out his wallet and emptied the contents on the desk. "You know what? I'm going to put my money where my mouth is. Two thousand dollars. I'm going to make you a bet."

Harrison grinned. "If I remember correctly, you've lost the last three wagers between us."

Greg shrugged. "They don't count. They were wagers on sports and business deals. This is a wager on everyday life—something, my friend, you don't know the first thing about—and knowing you as well as I do, there isn't a chance in hell I'm going to lose this time."

"Okay. Go for it. What's the wager?"

Greg picked up the money and waved it in the air. "I bet that you can't spend six weeks on your own. No servants. No mansion. Walk out into the real world and exist like everybody else. You wouldn't have the foggiest idea how to be a regular Joe."

"Six weeks?" Harrison mulled over the idea.

"You'll probably fall flat on your face in two days, but I'll tell you what I'll do. I'll lengthen it to eight weeks. Give you a chance to adjust so it's a fair try."

Harrison looked at him like he'd lost his mind, but he had to admit he found the idea intriguing.

Greg leaned back in his chair. "You criticize the women you meet for their interest in money and their search for security. Let's see how well *you* do in the big bad world without it. I bet it would change your attitude about some of the women who live in that real world full time."

Harrison's smile widened. "Maybe that's not such a bad idea. It's a deal. I'll take that bet."

Greg's grin froze on his face. "What? I wasn't serious. I was trying to make a point." His eyes widened. "You can't be considering it? There's no way you can walk away from all of this and survive."

"When you're right, you're right. I've had it easy my entire life. Yet I've always had a nagging feeling that I've been missing something. I've never known what. I think it's about time I found out."

Greg bolted from his chair. "I get it now." He laughed nervously. "You had me going there for a minute. We both know you can't go gallivanting around the country right now. We have a presentation due on our new design in ninety days."

"I'll be back in eight weeks, remember? And if something comes up and I'm delayed, you can handle it. The heavy lifting is already done." Harrison slapped Greg on the shoulder. "Besides, I'm not going far. I'm staying here in New Jersey."

"Here?"

"Yep. Some place I can be easily accessible if grandmother needs me in an emergency, but totally out of my social circle...someplace like...Trenton."

"Trenton?" Greg's face turned purple. "You need an automatic weapon and bullet proof windows just to drive down some of those streets."

The more Harrison considered the idea, the more appeal it had. "Not only am I going to do it," he said. "I'm going to sweeten the pot. I'll up the ante to one million dollars to be donated to the charity of your choice. And I'm going to throw in an additional challenge. I bet when I return in eight weeks I won't be alone. I plan to have my future wife by my side. And I'll know it's a union of love because she won't have a clue who I am until I return."

"A million dollars?" Greg's mouth hung open and he stared at Harrison as if he'd lost his mind.

"Don't worry. I'm not expecting you to ante more than the two thousand if I win. I'll make up the difference. Either way, one of our favorite charities will be the winner. And I'll pay you, personally, an extra hundred thousand to keep an eye on grandmother while I'm away."

"It was a joke! I never meant for you to take me up on it. Plus I can hold my own. If you put up a million, so will I. And since when do I have to be paid to keep an eye on *our* grandmother?"

Harrison sobered and stared long and hard at his friend. He'd unintentionally hit a sore spot. Since grandmother had adopted Greg when he was fifteen, he frequently got his back up if he thought he was looked at as an outsider. Harrison figured the best course of action would be to apologize. "Sorry, Greg. You know I didn't mean anything by it." He clapped his hand on his friend's shoulder. "But I'm getting really excited about this great idea of yours. I can't help wondering what I might have done with my life if I hadn't been blessed with the circumstances I was born into."

"You do plenty with your life. You run a multi-billion-dollar corporation. You donate heavily to charities. You provide scholarships to schools. You…"

"Don't you get it?" Harrison threw his hands up in the air. "What does it cost me if I have a hundred times the amount I donate still sitting in the bank?"

"I don't recall anyone turning down the donations."

"But what did I accomplish? What does it say about me?"

"That you're more generous than I am?"

"No! You're not listening." Greg's idea sounded better to him by the second. He'd been restless and bored lately. With the holiday season looming before them, things would be quiet at work. Besides he always closed the offices over Christmas week so his employees could spend time with their families. The timing of this venture couldn't be better. His pulse accelerated. Anticipation filled him with energy as he contemplated embarking on the adventure of a lifetime.

"Think about it." Harrison said. "What's the real measure of a man? Where does he find his strength? Build his character?" He slapped his hand on the desk. "It's in life's challenges. The hardships. The struggles. The way he responds is the measure of that man."

Greg's brow creased and a deep frown twisted his lips. "That cape is cutting off your oxygen supply. Let me call you a doctor."

Harrison grinned. "I'm not sick. Matter of fact, this is the best I've felt in a long, long time. What better way to find a woman to love me for myself and not my money than to date her when I don't have any?"

"Listen, I keep Dr. Stamper on speed dial for when I have a bout of depression or occasional crazies. Let me call her. You're losing it, man."

Harrison clasped his hands behind his head. "I'm going to do it. Think what an adventure it will be! In search of myself. In search of love. And I have you, my friend, to thank for it."

Greg's expression held a mix of angst and disbelief. "You can't be serious. You're going to fall flat on your face. Our business deal in Paris the first week of the new year is going to fail if you're not there. And you're thanking me? I think I'd better sell my stock while there's still time."

"Lighten up. This is exciting, challenging, fun!" His pulse raced, and he couldn't keep the silly grin off his face as he paced back and forth in front of the massive desk. "I might be only eight weeks away from marrying the love of my life."

"You mean eight weeks away from being carted off in a strait jacket."

"Lighten up. What are you worried about? You used to live in Trenton, didn't you? And you turned out just fine."

"That's exactly why I'm scared to death. I grew up on those streets. I've experienced poverty first hand and it isn't fun." Greg pounded his fist on the desk. "This isn't funny, Harrison. If it wasn't for your grandmother stepping in I would probably be dealing drugs or dead from them."

Harrison sobered. "Greg, I get it. I understand what you're saying. But most parts of Trenton are composed of middle-class neighborhoods filled with normal, hard-working middle-class people. I'm not going into the parts of town you're worried about."

"I should hope not. You wouldn't last five minutes on the streets.:

"Relax. It's going to be fine."

"Are you sure I can't talk you out of this craziness?"

"Aren't you the one who talked me into it? Since Greg looked like the veins in his neck were going to burst, he raised his hand in a calming motion. "It's going to be fine. Stop worrying. This was one of the best ideas you have ever had and I can hardly wait to get started. It's going to be an entire eye-opening experience for me...and one I am sure which will lead me to my true love."

A crisp rap on the door caught their attention and ended their conversation. A perfectly coiffed snow-white head popped inside. "I thought I might find the two of you in here." Patrice Stone opened the door wide, entered the room and pointed a heavily jeweled, wrinkled hand toward the stairs. "Let's go, boys. The auction is about to begin."

Two

Who would have imagined that grocery shopping could be so difficult?

Harrison had spent more than an hour pacing up and down the aisles trying to decide what to purchase—and even more importantly, how to cook what he had bought. It had never dawned on him when he started this adventure that he'd never prepared a meal for himself in his entire life.

Heck, he'd never had the need to even step inside a kitchen.

Walking into an actual grocery store had blown his mind. He hadn't the faintest idea where to go or what to buy. He'd ended up walking up and down the aisles endlessly until he settled on picking out fresh fruits and vegetables. Lots and lots of them. He figured he couldn't go wrong. He might turn into a rabbit before this adventure ended, but at least he wouldn't starve.

Harrison grinned. He supposed it was the shopping cart filled with mega amounts of veggies and fruit that had caught the produce guy's attention. Thank God, it had. Harrison saved face by playing macho man and explaining to the clerk he was setting up a bachelor pad. The man grinned and directed him to the frozen food aisle. Told him all he'd need was a microwave, and instructions on how to cook each meal were on the packages. So Harrison filled the rest of the cart with dozens of frozen dinners. None looked that appetizing. Certainly nothing like he was accustomed to eating. But it was only for eight weeks. He could survive eight weeks on frozen dinners, fruits, and salads. Piece of cake.

Now all he had to do was hope his apartment came with a microwave—and instructions on how to use it.

Harrison unloaded two moving cartons filled with clothes and household necessities from his trunk, then glanced down at the grocery bags. He'd had the cashier put his food items in plain brown paper bags so he could use them for trash or other needs and wouldn't have to buy trash bags. He grinned. Already thinking frugally about how to spend the small amount of cash he'd brought with him on this endeavor.

He glanced over his shoulder toward the apartment foyer.

Yep, he could make it. What was it? A half dozen yards, max? He hefted the cartons and bags. Sure, they blocked his vision but he'd go slow and peer around the sides. He grinned. And Greg thought he couldn't manage in the real world.

Well, watch out world. Here I come!

"Mom!" Six-year-old Christopher Hartman yelled from the open doorway. "Hurry up. I'm gonna miss the bus."

"I'm coming." Olivia rushed to the door, a brown paper bag clutched in her hand. "It's not my fault somebody thought cookies made a better lunch than the peanut butter and jelly sandwich I packed. Of course, I don't have a clue what little monster sneaked into your lunch pack last night and switched things, do you?"

She smoothed her son's reddish-brown hair back from his forehead, then traced her index finger across the dusting of freckles sprinkled across his nose. They mirrored the freckles on her own face. She had hated her freckles as a child, sometimes still did, and she couldn't help but wonder if her son did, too.

"Ahhhh, Mom."

"Okay, okay. Let's go."

They rushed to the bus stop together and got there not a moment too soon. Christopher boarded the bus and found a window seat. She waved to him as the bus pulled away. He was growing up so fast. She kept reminding herself to cherish every moment, even the rushed, yucky ones, because it wouldn't be long before he wouldn't want her going to the bus stop with him anymore.

Before turning back toward her apartment, she stole a moment to enjoy the fall morning. The last brilliant splashes of reds, oranges, yellows, and greens adorned the trees before the upcoming onset of winter. Even the drab brick apartment complex looked revitalized against the colorful backdrop. A walk in the park would be great. Crisp, cool air filling her lungs while her sneaker-clad feet slammed against the soft nature trail as she jogged.

For a split second she almost gave in to the urge, but the sane, responsible mom put a quick stop to the daydream. Being a single mom meant she had no one to share the responsibilities with and today's 'to-do' list was longer than her arm.

But this had been her choice. She could still hear her mother's voice in her head.

You need to give this child up for adoption. What kind of life can you possibly provide? Look at you! You're a high school dropout. A failure. You can't take care of yourself. What makes you think you can take care of a baby?

Every now and then—usually when she was tired or short of money, which was often lately—her mother's words hit home and made her question her ability as a mom. Made her wonder if her son would have been better off with both a mother and a father in a middle or upper class house, in an better lifestyle, one she would never be able to provide.

But doesn't everybody have tough times, wealthy or not? Brad and Angelina got a divorce. Ben Affleck and Jennifer Garner. Yep, even fame and fortune doesn't save you from hard times.

Determined to shake off negative feelings and replace them with happy, uplifting thoughts like her motivational tapes taught her, Olivia stole one last moment to enjoy the outdoors. With a smile on her face and a bounce in her step, she hurried back inside.

Less than an hour later a loud, persistent buzzing pulled her away from finishing the breakfast dishes.

No! No! No! Not again!

Olivia stared at the small apartment-sized stackable washing machine.

Would it kill you just once to finish the spin cycle without a tantrum?

Olivia held her breath, lifted the lid, and stared into the tub of stagnate dirty water.

"C'mon, honey, you can do it," she whispered to the machine.

She redistributed the weight of the clothes, lowered the lid, and pulled out the restart dial. The machine's buzzer sounded again, giving a raspberry to the silly human who hoped coddling and sweet words would change the inevitable, and it refused to spin.

Olivia's shoulders sagged beneath a heavy sigh. A repairman was not in this week's budget. Looked like a trip to the laundromat took front and center on her 'to-do' list. Well, might as well make the most of it. She twisted the excess water out of the clothes and tossed them in a basket.

If I'm stuck going to the laundromat, I might as well make the best of it.

She gathered the remaining dirty clothes from the hamper, swung by Christopher's room to grab his discarded Superman pajamas that had served as his Halloween costume, and threw everything into a second basket. Rummaging in her purse for loose coins, she counted what she found and rummaged some more.

Not enough.

Never enough.

Olivia shot a glance at the glass jar with a tag that read "Disney World" on the kitchen counter. This wasn't the first time she'd needed to dip into it for emergencies. She'd been doing it a lot lately. She'd have to find a creative way to answer Christopher if he asked why the money in the jar wasn't getting any higher. Her conscience blasted her with slings and arrows. Stealing from her kid's dream vacation jar.

What kind of mother was she? The kind of mom who wanted to send her kid to school with clean, dry clothes. She shook off the negative thoughts and replaced them with a positive plan. She'd ask Tony for an extra shift at the restaurant and put whatever tips she got right back into the jar. With any luck she'd put in more than she'd taken out.

Besides, things were about to change. She'd found a great audio book at the library on dating and she intended to follow the instructions to a tee. It was time she started dating again. Might as well date a guy with a good job and some money in the bank. Just because she was poor didn't mean the men she dated had to be poor, too. And this book was going to teach her how to do it. How to put herself in the right spots to meet men with money. How to dress correctly and act properly so she'd attract them to her. The tape suggested learning a sport, like tennis or golf, to put herself in proximity of the kind of men she wanted to date. She could take lessons for tennis at the YMCA. Couldn't hurt, right? And she was great at miniature golf. How hard could regular golf be?

Yeah, that's what she'd do. Take lessons and broaden her dating horizons. See, she felt better already and she was only on chapter two of the book.

A smile pulled at her lips.

Christopher needed a good male role model in his life and it was time she did something about it. And, yes, she had to admit she missed having someone to share her life with—and her bed. Heat seared her cheeks at the thought. Well, why not admit it? Sometimes she got lonely. Sometimes she ached to feel a man's arms wrapped around her or a strong, muscled chest to nestle her head against in bed.

So shoot me! I'm human.

Sudden tears burned the back of her eyes, but she refused to acknowledge them. Sometimes doing everything alone was so hard. But she had no time for a pity-party. She had plans. Plans for a brighter future for both of them. All she had to do was keep on track.

She attached her old MP3 player to her belt and pushed her long hair aside to slip the buds in her ears. Turning on her book-on-tape, she slid her cell phone into her jeans pocket along with her keys, picked up the two cumbersome laundry baskets, stepped out into the apartment foyer, and struggled to pull her door closed. When she heard the click, she turned and wham!

What the...?

She'd collided with something. Big. Hard. Immovable. The impact knocked her off balance and she dropped her baskets. On instinct she reached out to grab something to keep from falling. A loud rip sounded and she found herself tumbling to the floor in spite of her efforts to prevent it. Olivia glanced at the piece of brown paper bag clenched in her fist and then looked up at the tall stranger towering over her. She must have torn the poor man's grocery bag open.

"I'm so sorry." She tossed the paper aside and scrambled on her knees across the floor, collecting his runaway produce. "I didn't see you." In her peripheral vision she saw her upturned laundry baskets and several items of wet laundry dotting the hall. It wasn't until she spotted one of her bras draped across a head of lettuce that she wanted the floor to open up and swallow her. Red hot heat scorched her cheeks as she snatched the embarrassing underwear.

"No apology needed," a deep, masculine voice replied. "It was my fault. Wasn't watching where I was going. I was trying to carry groceries on top of these moving boxes, which was stupid, and..." Strong fingers wrapped around her upper arm. "Here, let me help you up."

Olivia stood. Oranges, her bra, and her arm got wedged against her boobs as she tried to resist the man tugging on her. He was going to make her drop everything if he didn't stop pulling her toward him. She threw an angry glance his way and was just about to tell him to take his hands off of her when her tongue did a funny thing—it stayed still.

Olivia's eyes widened. What was a tall, broad shouldered guy, maybe six-foot-two, and a hunk to boot doing here? She hadn't seen anyone this handsome around here since...ever!

His navy-blue tee shirt beneath his jean jacket stretched across a broad chest and clung to a flat abdomen that screamed six pack before tucking into a pair of skin tight jeans. Her eyes rested on his belt buckle, and for a split second she was tempted to scan lower, until sanity snapped back in.

The man chuckled, the glint in his eyes letting her know he was well aware of her sizing him up. "Bet you never knew doing laundry could be this dangerous, did you?" He righted her laundry baskets. "I apologize. I wasn't watching where I was going."

"It's okay." The words came out in a breathy whisper. Her eyes widened even more. Did she really just do that? Sex goddess she wasn't. Was she insane trying to portray one? If she didn't get it together, she'd embarrass herself even more, if that was possible, by drooling all over the poor guy.

"In spite of what you might be thinking," the tall, gorgeous hunk said, "I'm normally not such a klutz. I didn't hurt you when I knocked you over, did I?" His smile seemed so genuine and friendly, it sent a warmth skittering along every nerve ending in her body.

What in the world was he doing in her foyer? And with moving boxes? Nah. Couldn't be.

"My name is Harri...uh, Harry." He stared intently at her head. "Can you hear me?" He gestured to her earphones.

"Sorry." She pushed the off button on the player on her belt and pulled her earbuds out. "Hi. I'm Olivia." She offered her hand and was surprised at how small it felt clasped in his grasp. His hands were smooth, not calloused, and his nails were trimmed and clean.

Okay, so he didn't get his physique from construction work.

"I suppose saying 'nice to meet you' is silly." She reclaimed her hand. As she bent to help him pick up more of his groceries and gather the rest of her laundry, she noted the sealed moving cartons. There were four entrances to apartment in this foyer. Hers. Next door was elderly Mrs. Smalley, and across the hall was a newlywed couple she rarely saw. Only one apartment could be unoccupied, but she wasn't sure. The man who lived there traveled frequently and she'd only caught glimpses of him coming or going.

"Are you moving in?" she asked.

"Yep." Trying to avoid another mishap, they danced carefully around each other gathering the rest of their fallen items. "I'm moving into Apartment C," he said, indicating the door behind him.

"Really? I didn't realize the man who lived there had moved. Shows you how observant I am." She smiled at him and for a moment got lost in the deep brown eyes looking back. She'd always had a sweet tooth for chocolate.

"He's on an extended business trip. I agreed to sublet from him while he's gone."

She nodded, like it was any of her business anyway. She felt embarrassed by both her nosiness and her uncharacteristic attraction to him. She'd been out of the dating game for a long time, but her reaction to this guy was ridiculous.

"Well, welcome to the neighborhood." Gathering the rest of her laundry, she turned to go.

"Wait! I think you're forgetting something."

She glanced over her shoulder and saw the man offering her a pair of her son's sopping wet jeans. Olivia placed the baskets on the floor again and took the pants. "Thanks. They're my son's. My washer went out just as it hit spin cycle. Ever have one of those days?" She chuckled mirthlessly and added the pants to her laundry.

"Uh…pardon me, but these don't belong to me either."

Forced to look in his direction again, she gasped aloud as she saw a pair of silk peach panties dangling from his index finger.

Buy now: https://www.amazon.com/Forever-Love-Billionaires-Diane-Burke-ebook/dp/B08GH5MGF2

Website: https://dianeburkeauthor.com

www.ingramcontent.com/pod-product-compliance
Lightning Source LLC
Chambersburg PA
CBHW071719140626
46557CB00012B/964